GW00363427

This book

POOLBEG

First published 1989 by
Poolbeg Press Ltd.
Knocksedan House,
Swords, Co. Dublin, Ireland.

This book is published with the assistance of
The Arts Council/An Chomhairle Ealaíon, Ireland.

ISBN 1 85371 050 4

Cover design by Steven Hope
Typeset by Print-Forme,
62 Santry Close, Dublin 9.
Printed by The Guernsey Press Ltd.,
Vale, Guernsey, Channel Islands.

BAKER'S DOZEN

BAKER'S DOZEN

Edited by
Clodagh Corcoran

POOLBEG

Contents

	Page
Close Shave *Nell McCafferty*	1
The Pebble *Bryan MacMahon*	19
A Summer's Day *Elaine Crowley*	37
Mister Thirteen *Robert Neilson*	51
Cloudchaser *Morgan Llywelyn*	75
The Footpath *Hugh O'Neill*	95

Page

The Tale of the Missing Mouse   125
  Dolores Walshe

Learning by Accident   139
  Carolyn Swift

The Picnic   169
  Anne Roper

Summers Are Best   189
  Michael Scott

The Longest Day   201
  Ita Daly

Struggles of a Storyteller   221
  Mary Beckett

Rosaleen Rafferty at
  Rosario's Tech   237
  Evelyn Conlon

Close Shave

Nell McCafferty

Close Shave
Nell McCafferty

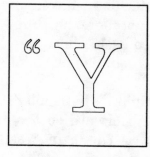

ou can have a go to
night. There's no dan-
ger you'll cut my throat
with this thing." Her father held out the new
electric razor and grinned at her. He had
changed out of his working clothes and stood
there now in a clean shirt. She rubbed the few
bristles on his face before she began.

"They don't feel the way they do in the
morning, Daddy."

"It'll be a long while before you're let shave
your father in the morning. I've got my
Adam's apple to protect. This is just to let you
get the feel of things. Now away you go, down
around the jaw, nice and easy. That's it.
That's it, love."

She cupped his chin in her left hand,
moving the machine round and round his

1

right cheek. It was magic, seeing the little hairs disappear. Crossing her right hand over the left, she attempted to shave his other cheek and fumbled. The machine whirred on the bone under his eye. "Hup, there, hip, hup, hup," he yelped and stepped back. She agreed to let him finish the job himself. She had a lot to learn yet.

"Now, what do you think?" he smiled, bending down and leaning forward so that she could stroke his face. The skin was smooth. He looked so clean. Magic. It had always been magic for her, watching his appearance change from dark to light, harsh to smooth, as he shaved. She wished that she could do that to herself. A girl couldn't take ugly things off her face. The most she could do was conceal them by putting on paint and powder. Then it would run and leave her blouse dirty. Her father's shirt was spotless as he left the house.

Later that evening, he smiled with delight when he saw her walk towards him along the edge of the football pitch. She was still wearing her school uniform. It marked her out as a clever girl, established him as a successful working man.

"Hello daughter," he said. He loved using those words, daughter or son. He introduced her to the other men in the group. She did not feel awkward. Her father's natural courtesy, and pride in his children, ensured that they were always at ease in his protective company. He had taught them to shake hands when they were introduced. She liked that ritual very much. She had noticed that extending her hand in greeting put adults at ease. It stopped them embarking on desperate baby-talk.

All the same, her heart was thumping. Her father, grinning with pride as he drew his student daughter into their company, had no idea of the shock she had in store for him, That it would be shocking she did not doubt. Her mother's reaction had prepared her for it. "You'll have to ask your daddy," she said. "It's up to him. Go on now. Don't be afraid. He won't eat you." If there was no need to be afraid, why was her mother afraid? Why couldn't her mother just say yes, and tell her father about it later? She had sensed her mother's humiliation in the kitchen, seen it in the stance of her body as she twisted the dish cloth in her hands, heard it in the cheerful, nervous exhortation.

Now, she stood on the edge of the football pitch, courage draining out of her, hatred beginning in her. On a balmy spring evening, in the space of an hour, her relationship with her father had changed. The loving man she had shaved was her master, and master too of her mother, his wife, whom he adored.

Her father was telling the other men the names of the subjects she was studying. He made the conversation easy for them, with charming self-deprecation, inviting them to shake their heads in wonder with him at the marvellous opportunities available now that had been denied all of them in their day. All of them, he stressed tactfully, bantering about how the headmaster had caned them for coming to school without pencils. "Sure we'd no chance," he said. "It's different now, with the free books and the grants and all." His beaming gaze belied his modesty. He was as proud as a man could be. It was obvious too that he relished his status there as father. No other children had come to the football field to stand with their fathers. His children, clearly, were not afraid of him.

Far from it. People used to remark how

they clustered round him in infancy. They were the only children in the neighbourhood who stood in the street waiting for their daddy to come home from work. The four of them, standing at the corner every evening, had become a kind of landmark, constant and reliable as Big Ben. If the McDaid girls and boys were at the crossroads, it must be six o'clock.

It always was. Their father always appeared in the distance at that time, cycling steadily, contentedly, home from work. He had a smashing smile. Jaunty, vain about his teeth, handsome perhaps, though she could not tell. She knew enough to tell that he loved them. His eyes became fond when he saw his brood. Later, when she understood such descriptions, she would understand what people meant when they described a small man as banty. "Bantam: a small variety of the domestic fowl; the cocks are spirited fighters." Later, when she understood that Catholic men in Northern Ireland would always be second-class workers, she would appreciate the spirited courage that brought this intelligent wee bantam cycling home with a smile on his face to his domestic flock. There he always was, their Daddy, rhythmic, constant as the seasons, on his bike. Coming home. Courteous, delighted, neighbourly, proud, looking forward to his children, his wife, his dinner, his home.

King, she realised now in the football grounds, of what little he surveyed and could control. Lovely, loving, generous, absolute King of all their crossroads.

He would dismount at the crossroads, push the cap back on his head, and steady his bicycle against the tumult of his children. He would kiss them, one by one. He was not like others. There was another daddy in her street, father of her best friend, and one evening he had staggered down it, drunk out of his standing. Her friend was devastated; the neighbours were tactful. What unemployed Irishman would not be drunk, once in a while, degraded, despite his skill, in a British colonial territory? Her father had helped the man fit his key into the front door.

At the crossroads her father would gather them onto his bicycle, putting one on the saddle, two on the cross-bar, one on the handlebars. He pushed them home, ringing the bell as he came alongside a neighbour, pretending exhaustion, exulting in his burden. Under the weight of the children, the bike wobbled but Daddy didn't miss a footfall. There was no fear that the machine would collapse under the weight of it all; there was a little discomfort as the crossbar bit between their legs, but he gave them each a chance on the saddle, remembering faultlessly each day whose turn it was now. He gave them lessons on the short journey home, challenging them to pronounce and spell the names of the streets they passed. Sober, hard-working, bantam of a daddy, devoted to his family, doing his best.

Sentimental nonsense, she thought now, standing in the football grounds, fifteen years of age, tired of hurting herself on the bar of his bike. It was time to tell him why she was there. Her fear made her dislike him. "Daddy," she said, "I want to go to a dance tomorrow night."

As presaged by the shadow on her mother's face, the face of her father darkened and became angry. She felt what her mother had involuntarily expressed one hour before, the stirrings of loathing. She knew from the look on his face that he would go home and blame her mother.

Blame her for what? What blame could be attached to a woman who recognised that the time had come for a girl to go dancing? What kind of man was he that his daughter should be made to feel bad about wanting to dance with men?

Assuming that any men would ask her to dance, she reflected sourly. Her father's fears were hugely misplaced. Standing there beside him in her ill-fitting gymfrock, pimples all over her face, fat flooding her thighs, she was hardly going to be the belle of the ball.

"Where is the dance?" he asked her.

"In the Savoy," she said, wishing the ground would open up and swallow her. The other men shifted quietly away from them, evincing sudden interest in the game. Everybody knew what went on in the Savoy. Sailors on shore-leave went there. There was nowhere else to go. The Savoy was the only dance-hall in town.

"Why tomorrow night?" he asked her.

"There's a great band coming. They're famous. It's their first time here. They mightn't be back for months.

"You can wait for a few months. You're only

fifteen. You're supposed to be at school, not trolloping around the town."

"I just want to dance, Daddy. Everybody else is going."

"And the money? Where do you think I'd get a ten-shilling note in the middle of the week?"

"Me mammy says it'll be all right. She says she'll give it to me."

"Did she now? Well, what are you asking me for then? The two of you have it all arranged, so what are you doing out here asking me?

"Can I go , Daddy?"

"Aye," he said, and he glared at her, and turned abruptly back to the match. She walked, quaking, out of the field and onto the road. She hated him, for frightening her like that. She turned back after a few steps, returned to the entrance, and sneaked a look at him. The bantam look had gone off him. His stance was sad.

She thought about her father on the way home, puzzled and mulling over the way they had both changed. She remembered the night she had worn her first bra. It belonged to her sister, and her mother had suggested that she try it on. When she came downstairs to the kitchen, wearing it under a heavy sweater, her father had risen gravely from his chair by the fire, come over to her, kissed her cheek and held her at arm's length. "You look lovely, daughter," he said. "Congratulations." He beamed all over his face. She believed him.

"We'll go up the town at the weekend and buy you one of your own," her mother said.

"I think I'll just go out for a walk," she said to them.

"Why wouldn't you, and you looking like a film-star?" her daddy said.

She had spent two hours roaming the streets, in the twilight, calling into corner shops to buy sweets, inviting admiration, spending her last sixpence on a record in the juke-box in the fish and chip shop. She selected "Blue Moon," and crooned quietly along with Elvis.

You saw me standing alone,
Without a dream in my heart,
Without a love of my own.

She did not feel alone. She felt charmed and beautiful. Her father had said so.

Now he had turned against her, and she

against him. She didn't care. She wondered, as she walked home, what the dance would be like. Little thrills pleasured her body. Her scalp tingled when she thought of walking finally through those doors, into the spotlights, ready for rhythm. A song her mother used to sing came into her head.

> *Put another nickle in,*
> *In that nickleodeon,*
> *All I want is loving you and music, music,*
>   *music.*
> *Closer, my dear come closer ...*

Next night her father sat beside the fire, his face thunderous. She stood on the hearthstone, looking into the mirror, and put lipstick on. She twirled mascara onto her eyelashes. Leaning closer she had to tuck her skirt between her legs to avoid the flames. Just as she prepared to apply panstick to her face, her father spoke.

"Get that muck off your face," he snarled. "No daughter of mine will go out of here looking like a tramp."

She caught her mother's eyes in the mirror, saw the quick shake of her head. She put the panstick back onto the mantlepiece.

"Well, I'm away now. Cheerio," she said.

"What time is the dance over?" her father asked.

"Eleven o'clock."

"Be you in home by quarter past," he said. He did not look at her. His voice was directed at the fire. Her mother left her to the front door.

"See and enjoy yourself," she smiled.

"Oh I will mammy," she said. They grinned at each other.

"But remember now, he means that about being home by quarter past."

Margaret was waiting outside the Savoy, the eyes dancing in her head. "Are you ready, Emer?" "I can't wait," she said, and she and Margaret walked through the great swing doors, past the bouncers, up to the cashier. They paid their money, walked stiffly along the foyer, a little nervous now, and turned into the cloakroom. The woman took their coats and gave them tickets.

"What do we do with our handbags, Margaret?"

"I don't know. See what everybody else is doing, I suppose."

They could hear the music in the distance. They pushed open yet another door and heat blasted into their faces. On the dance-floor couples swung and jived and contorted into fantastic shapes. The noise was tremendous. The band up on the stage glittered in their blue jackets, epaulettes, brass buttons and startingly white trousers. A huge golden globe hung from the ceiling. Coloured spotlights swept the floor and the crowds. Women stood at one side of the hall, men stood at the other.

As they made for the women, a man stopped Margaret and asked her to dance. Margaret gave her handbag to Emer, flashed her eyes with excitement, and stepped into glory.

Emer stood among the women all night long, clutching the two handbags. She could smell her own sweat, which she knew perfectly well was the smell of rejection. At a quarter to eleven a very small man came towards her. She had seen him work his way down the line of women, his face impassive as they each refused his invitation to dance.

His nickname was Snout. It was cruelly accurate. He had the face of a little pig. His body was stunted. His clothes were unclean.

She accepted his invitation with alacrity,
moving at last onto the floor, under the
beautiful globe. Both handbags hung heavily
from the crook of her left elbow as she
followed him to a clear space. They faced each
other, the music began, she raised her right
hand and stepped towards him.

Her hand stayed uncertainly in the air as
he placed his arms around her waist and
pulled her against him. They shuffled
untidily in a small circle, without grace or
rhythm. Her right hand lowered itself onto
his shoulder. The handbags on her left arm
bumped against their jointed elbows. He
forced his cheek against hers. It was sweaty,
smooth and smelly with sickly-sweet
aftershave.

They were dancing.

It was her first dance.

She was enthralled, enchanted as she gazed
over his shoulder, looking at handsome
people, ugly people, ordinary people, dancing
to the music of a famous band under the
beautiful globe. It was the last dance.

Margaret rushed over as the music died,
grabbed her handbag from Emer, said they
should try and be first into the cloakroom for

their coats, and ran for the door. "Did you enjoy it?" she grinned as they pushed through to the counter.

"It was magic," said Emer.

"See you in school. Oh God, it's five past eleven," Margaret shouted over her shoulder as they split outside the dancehall and ran in different directions.

Eventually Emer slowed down, out of breath. She wanted to dawdle, she wanted to dream. She started to walk. When she arrived at the crossroads, away from the city centre, she noticed how dark was the road home. There were three back-lanes between her and the street where she lived. She felt fear. A man might jump out of the back-lanes, grab her and do things to her. She had heard stories. All the girls in school had stories.

She prayed as she neared each narrow, black gash between the streets. Her heart was thumping again, as it had the night before when she approached her father in the football field. She wished Snout had asked to leave her home. She could have dumped him on her doorstep. She broke into a run as she neared a back-lane, whimpering, feeling foolish as she escaped what was not there, then grateful for the escape.

She arrived into the kitchen in record time.

Her father was waiting for her.

"You're late," he said angrily.

"It's only twenty past eleven," she said.

"Don't contradict me. I told you to come straight home. What have you been doing?"

"Nothing," she said.

"You spent all night doing nothing? Do you take me for a fool? You were out dancing and now you're late, and now you're lying to me. Don't you dare tell me you were doing nothing. You were out dancing."

"I got one dance from Snout."

His enraged face was close to hers. The certainty of it changed slightly. Everybody knew Snout. She saw that her father's skin was not smooth. There was a light stubble on it. Snout's skin had been smooth. At least he had shaved, to please her and any other girl. She wouldn't have minded, knowing what she knew now, if he had asked to leave her home. He would at least have gotten her safely past the back-lanes. She could have dumped him on her doorstep. And gone into the arms of her angry father.

"Goodnight," she said. She did not call him

Daddy. He did not answer. He did not call her daughter. He remained silently in the kitchen while she went upstairs.

She heard her mother's urgent whisper from behind the opened door of the bedroom where her parents slept.

"Did you enjoy yourself?"

"It was great, mammy."

"Sleep tight now, Say your prayers." She could hear the comforting chuckle in her mother's conspiratorial voice. She had a lot to learn yet. She fell asleep dead happy.

The Pebble

Bryan MacMahon

The Pebble

Bryan MacMahon

idway in the little waterfall which stre-amed over a low wall of rocks there was a breach through which the river water poured in a torrent that plunged boldly into the gravel-bedded pool below. Two girls, Peggy, seventeen and Nell, sixteen, lolled on the long summer grasses on a bank above the pool.

There came a pause in their laughing conversation. Each girl seemed to have retreated into her inmost thoughts. Also, it was as if the sound of the rushing water had made speech unnecessary. As close friends they understood the value of silence.

Small summer sounds were faintly heard: the sighing of leaves in the copper beech tree above them, the perfunctory barking of a dog in the sun-stilled distance. Suddenly, as the sound of a woman's voice was heard calling her name from far above the wood, Peggy came smilingly to her feet. "That will be my mother. Visiting your house. I've got to go. Coming, Nell?"

Languor lingered in Nell's eyes as she looked up. "It's lovely here," she said. "I'll stay a while."

"Don't stay too long. See you Sunday."

Moving swiftly Peggy went along the pathway that led upwards through the trees. Her mother's drawn-out cry of "Pegg-y" lent spurs to her heels.

When her companion had gone, Nell curled up lazily in the long grass. Her mind surrendered itself to the muted birdsong and the hum of bees amid the river-side flowers. She plucked lazily at the grass stems. She was sorry she had not brought along her bathing costume but then she recalled that she had been warned against swimming alone. Her eyes intuitively rested on the mid-stream chute, where as a child she had been brought in springtime to watch the silver salmon leap from the pool, battle with the torrent and, finally, win their way to calm water above the spawning beds far up-stream.

The movement of the water was mesmeric. Water, water flowing, flowing since the beginning of time until now. And further still into a future of unreckonable ages.

Suddenly Nell's eyes tightened. She raised herself slightly on to her elbow. In the flat water above the falls she saw the dark head of a young man swimming downstream and heading calmly but resolutely for the midstream breach in the cascade. The girl lowered her head but continued to watch through the long grass stems. She was fully alert now.

With a cry of triumph the boy, for at seventeen or eighteen he was little more than that, swam strongly onto the current of the breach, shot fluently through the white water and dived deep down into the pool. After what seemed to the girl a long interval his head came up close to the point where the water tailed off before gathering momentum for another downward plunge. As his head came up he shook the water from his short black hair and gave a cry of delight and freedom that echoed through the woods.

Nell's heart beat faster. She tried to crouch still lower on her couch of grass. She glanced sidelong to find a means of escape. There was a wiggle of concern in her eyes. In the flash of time during which she had watched him slide through the torrent she could not help seeing that the boyman was wearing nothing at all.

Don't stir, she told herself, now feeling somewhat like a young rabbit in the presence of a stoat. He hasn't seen me yet. Perhaps he will swim downriver. Carefully, inch by inch, she raised her head. He was standing waist deep in the water just below her. And looking upwards.

"Hello!" he shouted.

(Lie low. Do not answer, the girl told herself.)

"You up there. Hello."

Nell raised her head a little. The water had combed his short black hair down over his forehead. It glistened and gleamed on his fine body. He had mocking but piercing blue eyes. She had never seen him before. Probably a visitor to one of the farms further up the river. Nell wished Peggy had not gone; then vaguely she was glad that her companion had left her.

"The water is lovely. Come for a swim."

A swim with him? And he as he had come into the world. A bold rascal indeed!

She raised her head. Her eyes were elsewhere than upon him. Primly, "No thank you."

"Why not?"

"Why do you think?"

"All I think is that it is July. The day is warm and the water clear."

Nell placed her hand on the grass for leverage to help her rise.

"Afraid?" he taunted.

"Of you?"

"Of me, yes. You needn't be. I won't harm you. I won't even touch you." He laughed. "It is not good for man to be alone."

Nell was on her feet now. With head averted she gave an uncertain laugh. "I've no..." she began. She asked herself if her sense of outrage was faked or not,

Calmly "Neither have I." There was a pause. Then "Are you like Fial?"

"Fial?"

"You don't know about Fial?" His chaffing tone of voice stopped her as she was about to go. "She's the lady for whom this river is

named. F-i-a-l, Fial. In English it's spelt
F-e-a-l-e, Feale."

Nell looked down with what she hoped was
amusement, if not sarcasm.

"Thousands of years ago she drowned in
this river," he went on. "Maybe in this very
pool. D'you want to know why she drowned?"

Nell shrugged as if it didn't matter.

"She died of shame," the boy said matter-of-
factly.

"Of shame?"

"Needless shame. A summer's day just like
this. Fial stepped down the pathway through
the trees. She was the most beautiful woman
in the Ireland of her day. She stood just where
you are now. Looked about her and listened.
No-one to be seen. Nothing to be heard but
birdsong and the sound of falling water. She
came down that little pathway to the water's
edge. Behind the trailing branches of that
beech tree, or one like it, all her summer
clothes slid from her body. Her full beauty
was now to be seen. She opened the curtain of
the leaves. Paused to listen again. Dived into
the water. She swam like an otter. Came up
just there …Can you swim?"

"Of course."

"Don't go! I'm not finished ... After a time Fial made to return to the tree. She heard a twig snap underfoot. She looked up. A short distance above, among the trees, a man was watching. The sun was in Fial's eyes but she had seen enough to make her panic. She dived back into the pool. Down down she went. Came up. The man was there. Still watching. Again she dived, downstream this time to where the pool is far deeper. She was overcome by shame. The man walked down to the river's edge.

"'Fial,' he called. 'It is I ... your husband, Lugh,' Fial did not answer. She could not answer. She had drowned of needless shame."

Nell stood still, half interested, half amused.

"What's your name?" the boyman asked in a gentle tone of voice.

"Ellen — they call me Nell."

"I'll call you Fial. In my own mind. Now that I've told you the story, will you come into the water?"

"No."

"Why not?"

"You're not my husband."

His response was a guffaw. "If that's all, I'll

marry you."

"You'll marry *me*?"

"Fair and square. Church, bell, book and candle."

Half jokingly from Nell, "How can I be sure?"

"I'll give you a token." As she turned to go, "Wait," he shouted.

He dived down fully into the depths of the pool. She could see the faint glow of his body on the riverbed. When again he surfaced, his left hand had closed to a fistful of pebbles. Standing waist deep he selected one pebble from those on his palm then rinsed his hand of the rest. The selected pebble was brown and white in colour and irregular in shape. It was about the size of a fingernail. Nesting it on the thumbnail of his right hand and bracing it against his index finger, "Catch!" he shouted as he flicked the pebble upwards to where the girl was standing. Nell caught it against her breasts. She looked from the pebble to the smiling young man below.

"You joking?" she asked earnestly.

"I'm steadfast," he said in a calm sure tone of voice.

This was crazy, Nell told herself. Wisdom

and prudence called on her to run off. Yet, the word steadfast enticed her to stay. Strange the power of a word, she mused; at times it can alter the course of a whole life. She stood irresolute. What she was being tempted to do was utterly forbidden in that place and in that day. If she was discovered, her name would be a by-word among the people. "Nell is loose," she could already hear the whisper of evil gossip in the countryside. Like Fial she, too, would die of shame.

And yet, below her was the young man standing in the water, his hands on his hips, seemingly quite confident that he would win this natural combat of wills. Beneath his feet the bed of the river was crazy-paved with shifting tiles of light. The water hissing over the rock wall seemed to repeat the word "steadfast." Sssteadfast! She knew the word meant constant, unwavering, firm, true. Her fist tightened about the pebble. Tightened until her fingers ached. Then, "I promise," the boyman said calmly. "I won't even touch you." After a moment or two of silence "Go on. There's only us."

Before she fully realized what she was doing, Nell was stepping down the narrow path to the little mound of white gravel curtained by the trailing tendrils of the copper beech tree. Where she stood now was a natural room for robing — or disrobing. "Sssteadfast" the water continued to murmur in quiet sibilance. "Turn away," she called out as her light summer clothes slipped from her body. The young man smiled and turned away. Nell was through the curtain and into the water — the young man turned and saw that the girl could swim like an otter. As he cupped his hand and splashed her the girl screamed, in joy and fear.

Keeping their distance from each other they played in the pool as Adam and Eve must have done before the Fall. Twisting, diving and breasting the current where it was strongest, the dark head and the fair, the dark body and the fair, in the urgency of apprehension and delight, matched and laughing together in the trust and comradeship of innocence, eagerness and freedom. They could even have been a pair of otters playing in the dawntime of creation.

Suddenly above the brawling of the water, Nell heard a call from behind the wooded clifftop far above — her mother was calling in the cows for the afternoon milking. The girl signalled an end to the play: she gestured him to look away while she was leaving the water. He dived deep as she left the pool and quickly drew aside the rustling curtain of the beechroom. With her fingertips she brushed the surplus water from her body and when he surfaced again she watched him through the whispering leaves.

He, too, was watching from the lower end of the pool. Seemingly out of nowhere a breeze came up and for a fleeting moment it stirred the curtain of the robing room. The girl was binding her hair at the nape of her neck when the young man remotely sensed her in the glory of first womanhood. The breeze died almost as soon as it sprang to life.

Nell dressed herself hastily. Her mind in confusion, she ran like a fawn up the pathway. As she was almost lost among the trees, "Fial" the boyman called from below. Nell turned, her face contrite. Raising his right hand "Steadfast," he shouted. His call echoed, re-echoed in the woods. Her fist clasped about the pebble, the girl turned and resuming her upward racing and was lost from his sight among the trees.

Six years passed. Peggy and Nell had woven their way through young loves and disenchantments. Peggy was almost engaged to be married but Nell was not. Her eyes were apt to grow pensive whenever the brown and white pebble showed up amid the glitter of her oval trinket box. She had fully confided in her companion. Of the young man of the incident in the pool she had heard nothing — she did not even know his name. Seeing the remoteness stealing into her companion's gaze, Peggy tried to tease Nell out of the recollection: if they were walking together along a freshly gravelled pathway Peggy had only to stop and stir the pebbles with the toecap of her shoe as if in search of a particular pebble to evoke a spurt of rueful laughter from her comrade. Still, by tacit consent, both agreed that six years was a long time to have a remote love-ache. Sensing this ache in her daughter, her wise mother said softly. "Be old-fashioned and patient, child, and you're bound to win."

At a crowded disco in a seaside resort as the pair stood by the wall, Nell suddenly gripped her friend's arm. "There he is," she said with urgency.

"Who?"

"The dark fellow with the fringe. Down there second from the end. He's ...

"Steadfast?" Peggy finished.

"I'd know him anywhere." Nell was breathless with excitement.

"What are you going to do?"

"Nothing."

"If I were you ..." Peggy had broken off as the young man moved to ask a partner to dance.

The lights. The music. The drumbeats found an answering echo in Nell's heart. She continued to stand still, the rhythm in her blood, the coloured lights on the now thronged floor finding and losing her face and form. A shift in the dance movement brought the young man and his partner still closer to her. No longer a boy, he was now in the fulness of manhood. Tall, broad, and with a fine carriage. He danced well. As if the intensity of her gaze had found him he turned his head so that for a moment his eyes met hers. Had he seen her? she asked herself. Had her smile of recognition been too casual or too eager? A friend asked her to dance; at first she was

tempted to offer an excuse but then she
accepted. It would prove that she was not a
leftover and there was the added bonus that
again his eyes might rest upon her in fuller
recognition. She danced as she swam — both
activities sprang from the depths of her
nature. Her eyes continued secretly to search
the throng to catch a glimpse of the young
man of the waterfall.

Later, as Peggy and Nell rested, they could
find no trace of the young man. Had he gone
off, as he had gone off six years before? The
music resumed its insistent beat. The drum
roll scorned denial. Couple after couple took
the floor.Whirl after whirl in harmony with
the mood of the summer night. "Found and
lost" — Nell's heart sank as she repeated the
words. "Be patient and you'll lose," she added
as if retorting to an absent mother.

Suddenly he was at her elbow having
emerged from the comparative darkness at
the other end of the hall. A gesture of
confident request from his open hands. She
hoped that her murmur of acceptance
sounded calm. Fluently away then. Taking
the rhythm from each other without flaw or

hesitation.

Whenever he touched her it seemed utterly right. Faster, still faster. Retreat and advance. Dancing together it was as if the two were already one. *I shall not be the first to talk*, Nell told herself despite her inner turmoil.

I shall not be the first to recall the pool — the resolution was implicit in the young man's proud eyes. *Also she gives me no opening to recall that summer day.*

A few desultory remarks as the dance ended. He escorted the girl part of the way to where Peggy, her face full of questions, stood waiting. "Thanks," he said curtly.

"A pleasure," she said, equally so. Was this truly an end to the dream? the young woman asked herself. She felt wounded and rejected as he turned away. Peggy had begun to blurt a question. She stopped in mid-sentence on seeing that the young man had turned as on a sudden resolution and was now standing facing her companion.

"Still got it?" he shot.

"What?" from Nell.

"The token."

"Token!"

"The pebble," he said.

After a pause, "Yes."

"You have it?"

"I have it, yes."

He laughed so loudly that the bystanders turned. "Nothing for it now," he said, "but to ..."

"To what?" from Nell.

"To marry you, of course."

"Just like that."

"Just like that! After all, six years is a long engagement."

Nell's eyes narrowed. "Still steadfast?" she asked in a low voice.

"Still steadfast," he said. "And you?"

The girl nodded.

"That settles it so," he said.

Nell had no need to answer. Her eyes brimmed with happy tears. Neither the young man nor the young woman needed to look elsewhere than at each other. They had been together overlong in thought alone.

A short time later before the wedding he asked her to return the pebble. Nell gave it to him without hesitation. During the marriage ceremony, at which Peggy was bridesmaid, he gave it back to her. The pebble was now set in gold and hung from a thin gold chain. A diamond sparkled on the single plane on its irregular surface. On the back of the token the words "To Fial from Lugh" were inscribed.

After the ceremony, still showered with confetti, as they were alone for the first time, he hung the token formally about her neck. Standing back and with his head to one side so to assess the effect it created, he laughed uproariously: he was obviously recalling the unconventional manner of their first meeting. As a slight frown crossed her face he took her in his arms and kissed her.

"Now, you need never drown of needless shame," he teased, "for you will swim like an otter in the pool of our love."

Nell smiled. She thought it prudent, for just this once, to let Mr Steadfast have the last word.

A Summer's Day

Elaine Crowley

A Summer's Day
Elaine Crowley

annah and I sat on the curb making poles of the summer dust that collected in the gutter and planning to murder John-Joe Durkin. John-Joe was three and a half and I hated him. He was small and pale, the front of his trousers was always wet and he kept kicking over our carefully made mounds of dust.

"After we murder him we'll chop him up in bits," I explained to Hannah and she agreed. A dray went past on its way to Fitz's pub. Great big horses pulled it. Horses nearly as big as the elephants in the zoo. Long hair grew round their hooves, almost touching the ground. One lifted its tail and steaming dollops of manure fell onto the road. As if by magic, bluebottles and flies appeared.

Murdering John-Joe was forgotten as Hannah and I found two sticks, ran into the road an upended the shiny brown balls from which pieces of undigested bran poked. The disturbed flies flew away.

"Get off this road before I tell your mothers," a passing woman shouted. If she did, which she might, my mother would be roaring and shouting from the window for me to come in and threatening what she would do to me when I did. So I said to Hannah, "we'll go and watch the barrels going down the hole."

"Alright," she said and we followed the dray to the public house. John-Joe started whingeing to come with us but I wouldn't let him.

The grating was up and the men in aprons were already lowering the barrels into the cellar. It was very dark down there. I stood near the edge and peered over. Thick dust lay like dirty grey wool and sweet papers and Woodbine packets lined the walls. The smell of porter was everywhere.

"Mind outta the way or youse'll be kilt," said a man in an apron. We ignored him. "Get outta the bloody way before I clatter the pair of youse."

"I know," I said to Hannah when the man threatened us again, "we'll go down the Alley and have adventures."

The Alley was a narrow lane which ran along the back of my side of the street. The shopkeepers threw their rubbish there. Sometimes there was treasure in the rubbish. Once I found half a crown. And my mother said "May God bless you, that's after getting me out of a hobble." Apples and oranges were thrown in the Alley, only a bit mouldy sometimes.

"I'll get into trouble if I go in the Alley again," Hannah said.

"Ah come on. Only for a few minutes. Sure your mammy won't know," I coaxed.

"No. I can't. Me mammy says I stink of fish when I've been in the Alley."

"Well, anyway, I'm going. And if you tell I'll scrawb your eyes out."

I ran off and left her.

The Alley was cool and dark. Battered ashcans overflowed. The Alley smelled of over-ripe fruit and rotten fish. I poked about looking for something or anything. A half empty vinegar bottle lay on its side amongst a patch of stinging nettles. I picked it up, pulled out the cork and drank it. I loved the sharp taste. My mother said you shouldn't drink vinegar, it dried your blood. A child she knew that drank vinegar had a terrible end— all dried up, her body like a sheet of brown paper. I didn't care. I drained the bottle and threw it over the wall.

Half way down the Alley was a hill, only a small one. I climbed up and sat on the top. Pee-the-beds grew there and nestling amongst the yellow flowers and ginny joe seed heads that you could tell the time by how many puffs it took to blow away all the seeds, was a dead fish. It must have been there a long time. The skin was coarse and dry. I turned it over with my foot. The underneath was moist. I poked a stick through, breaking the skin, and saw thick white maggots wriggling. The fish looked like a moving rice pudding.

Hannah had changed her mind. I could see her now timidly walking down the Alley, carefully stepping over the rotting vegetables. I hooked the stick inside the fish and flung it towards her. Clumps of maggots flew through the air. The fish missed her, hit the wall and landed on her white runners. She started to cry. "I'll tell my mammy so I will. I won't play with you anymore." She ran sobbing from the Alley. On top of my hill I danced and chanted, "Cry baby, cry baby." I was sorry when she went and stopped singing. Then consoled myself that after dinner we would make friends again. I'd send someone to ask if she was, "spin spout, or black out." If she said spin spout we would be friends. But if the answer was black out I'd have to try again.

I climbed down the hill and started for home. I walked slowly with my eyes down looking for treasure. Two seagull feathers lay on the tarry road. I dashed into the road and picked them up. Now I could play Indians. As I neared my hall door John-Joe sidled up. I stuck the feathers in my hair and did a war dance. His vacant pale eyes bulging like gooseberries stared at me. I stuck my tongue out and raced up the stairs.

My mother was at the gas stove cooking the dinner. "Where have you been? And what's that you have in your hair?" she asked looking around at me. "I've been calling you for hours. I've never met such a child in my

life. You're never where you should be. Where
were you?" She didn't really expect an answer
so I kept quiet and went to the window to
watch for my father who would be coming
home in a minute. I moved the lace hangings
to get a better view.

"Leave the curtains alone," my mother
shouted looking around again from the stove
and this time noticing the feathers in my
hair.

"What's that you have in your hair? take it
out."

"It's only two feathers. I was playing
Indians."

"I'll give you Indians—take them out
immediately."

I raised my hands and pulled at the
feathers. They fell forward over my face, the
quills bending, but the ends remained stuck
in my hair glued in by tar. "Will you take
them things out of your hair. You've been
down the Alley! Look at the cut of you! And
wash your hands—they're like pig's paws.
Take them out. How many more times do I
have to tell you," my mother's voice was
louder.

I tried again to pull out the feathers,

pulling hard wincing at the pain in my scalp. My mother crossed the room, looked at my hair and hit me a stinging slap. "Sweet Jesus what have you done to your hair—it's full of tar." A smell of burning filled the room. The drained potatoes left over the flame to dry had caught. She ran back to the cooker and removed the saucepan while still giving out about my hair. "You've destroyed it. What am I going to do with you. I'll kill you so I will." She got the big pair of scissors and came towards me, cut the feathers out of my hair, snapped them and threw them onto the fire. "Let me catch you putting anything else in your hair and see what you'll get."

Clouds of blue smoke began to fill the room. The frying pan had overheated and the smell of burning fat filled the air. "Now look at what you've been the cause of and your father walking in the door," she said and slapped me again. The more I cried the more she hit me. I cried louder hoping my father was coming and would hear me. "Stop that crying," she shouted. "Stop it, d'ye hear me." Then with a final slap she pushed me away saying, "now you've got something to cry for." Her face was creased and red and her eyes glared.

"I hate you, I hate you. I wish you were dead," I said again and again to myself.

"That's him coming now," said my mother. "Stop that crying before he comes in." I cried louder. My father would be on my side. He loved me the best.

He opened the door and the blue haze enveloped him. "What happened?" he asked.

"What happened is that that one came in full of tar and feathers. Look at it. Look at the state of her hair." She banged the iron pot on the stove trying to dislodge the burnt potatoes. "And it's all your fault," she continued. "You have her ruined. I can't get good of her.

"She's only a child. You're always on at her."

I sidled up to him, rubbing my face against his sleeve, forcing out the sobs. His coat smelled lovely. He ran his hand over my hair.

"Sit down and leave your father alone," my mother ordered. "Sit down now this minute."

My father had the top potatoes which hadn't scorched. Some of mine were burned but I liked the crispy bits. My mother as always had only a little dinner on a saucer. After the meal I asked, "Mammy, can I go down and play?" "Wait first and have a cup of tea, it'll be drawn in a minute."

Her anger was forgotten. She cut bread and buttered it, talking to my father at the same time. I ate bread and jam and sipped hot tea. My father gave her five shillings, tips he had made, and me two pence.

"Now can I go?" I asked again, finishing the last of my bread. She was engrossed in what my father was telling her, looking happy, smiling at him. "Yes," she said, "go down but stay where I can see you."

I shouted my agreement and I went through the door, raced down the stairs and out into the sunlit street, the slaps, the tears, tar and feathers all forgotten. John-Joe was sitting on the curb by the shore dropping stones into the water. I sat beside him, pushing him up a bit so I could throw stones into the grating too.

"Have you seen Hannah?" I asked. He shook his head; sometimes he answered you, sometimes he didn't. "Will you go to her house for me?" He looked sullen and shook his head again. "Ask her is she's spin spout or black out, go on."

"I won't," he said.

I gave him a good, hard shove and he started to cry. I stood up and ran away shouting. "John-Joe Durkin is no good. Chop him up for firewood."

I wandered down the street stopping to look in the shop windows, deciding how to spend my twopence. In the end I settled for Ma Doyle's toyshop where I bought a gelatine doll and a balloon on a bamboo stick with red feathers on the mouthpiece. When I came back there was still no sign of Hannah. If she didn't come soon I'd be stuck with John-Joe for the rest of the day.

I sat beside him and started to blow up my balloon. I blew hard and the red rubber swelled, the colour paled and the balloon grew into a big rose pink ball. I took it out of my mouth. The air rushed from it with a squeaking sound. John-Joe laughed and reached for it. I turned away from him and started blowing up the balloon again. John-Joe clapped his hands as it grew bigger and bigger.

"Me have it, me have it," he chanted, pulling at my arm. I stood up trying to shake him off but he clung on pulling harder on my arm. I jerked it to dislodge him. The balloon shot out of my mouth and sailed onto the middle of the road squeaking as it went. It landed and did a lot of little hops as the air escaped. John-Joe with a squeal of delight ran after it and straight into the path of a speeding sand lorry.

His body was lifted and thrown towards the grating. He fell with his head hitting the curb and his blood the same colour as the balloon ran down the drain. All the people came running from everywhere. Mrs Durkin came running down the street screaming. I ran away, around the corner and into the Alley. I climbed the hill and lay down in the grass that grew near the top of the wall.

I kept seeing John-Joe's blood going down the drain. He was dead and Hannah would tell everyone I had murdered him. My mother would kill me. I still had the gelatine doll. One of its legs dangled on the elastic thread. I pulled it off and threw it away.

I lay for a long time. It seemed a long time anyway. It began to get dark. My mother would be looking for me, calling me. She might think I was dead and be sorry for me. I was very hungry and wanted my tea. I pulled some stalks of grass and chewed them. I wanted to go home. But I couldn't. I could never go home again. I would have to stay here all night. I would be put into prison and have bread and water for ever and ever.

I sat up and looked down the Alley. It was nearly dark now. Cats were prowling, searching for fish heads. Two started to fight, spitting and snarling at each other. I thought about the dead fish I had thrown at Hannah and imagined the maggots crawling up the hill to eat me.

Then I heard the whistle. It was my father whistling the way he did to call me in. Then I heard him call my name. His footsteps came nearer. I could see him now. My sobs grew louder, each one hiccuping through my body, choking me so that I couldn't call out. He saw me and started up the hill. "Thank God, oh thank God, I've looked everywhere for you." He wrapped me in his coat and carried me down the hill. I clung to him and cried all the way home.

My mother was at the hall door. She ran to meet us. "Thanks be to God you're alright." She rubbed my hair where the feathers had been and hurried us up the stairs, saying, "Where were you? I was demented not knowing where you were." She talked all the time while she made me hot milk, repeating her fears and worries for my safety. "Tell her what happened to John-Joe, Mammy," my brother said. "Tell her Mammy." I closed my eyes. I didn't want to hear. I squeezed them shut. Maybe she'd think I was asleep, take the mug from my hand and carry me into bed.

"Poor little John-Joe," she said. "But wasn't he lucky all the same."

I opened my eyes. "What happened to him?" I asked.

"He was knocked down after dinner. But someone was praying for him. His head was split open, fourteen stitches, though thanks be to God he's going to be alright."

The mug slipped from my fingers onto the hearth, smashing, the milk trickling across the oilcloth. The cat lapped it.

"Why the hell can't you be more careful. I never knew such a child, always smashing and breaking something.

Everything was alright. I was home. I was safe. Everything was normal. "I'm tired," I said. "I want to go to bed."

Mister Thirteen

Robert Neilson

Mister Thirteen

Robert Neilson

illy was a good kid, really. He obeyed his parents, showed respect for his elders and kept his room tidy. Sometimes he even helped his mother around the house. But despite all these good qualities he managed to get himself into trouble. In fact it was his willingness to help that sort of led to his problem.

One evening after dinner Billy was helping his Mum clear the table. As he reached out to lift his father's plate his sleeve caught the side of the salt cellar and knocked it over. He carefully brushed the spilled salt into a little pile and swept it off the table into the palm of his hand. Then he walked to the kitchen, without spilling a grain on the diningroom carpet, and marched to the bin to dispose of it.

"Billy," his mother said. "You should throw a pinch of the salt over your shoulder for luck."

"Sure, Mum," he replied absently, dumping the salt into the bin and wiping his hands on a tea-towel. "I should throw some over my left shoulder with my right hand or I'll turn into a frog, or something."

"Don't make fun of things you don't understand, Bill," his Dad shouted from the diningroom where he still sat, finishing a cup of tea and reading the evening paper.

Billy put on a frown and deepened his voice. "If you make faces the wind will change and leave you like that." He giggled, realising how like his father that sounded. He continued in his normal voice. "This is the Twentieth Century folks. They stopped believing in witches and magic and that sort of stuff years ago."

"Don't talk like that to your mother, Bill," his Dad called. "You apologise right now," he ordered in that tone that says: or else.

"Okay, Okay! I'm sorry. But I still think that all this superstitious stuff is real rubbish."

The boy retreated rapidly upstairs to his

room. He had a geography project to finish for school the next morning and if it wasn't finished he'd get it from old Rhino — who Billy was sure had taken up teaching because he hated children. As he worked best in silence the radio stayed firmly off even though he fancied some music. Even the faint noise of the T.V. from downstairs distracted him sometimes. Oh well, he promised himself, the folks are going out tonight, so if I get this finished early enough I'll be able to watch Monsters of Rock. He set to his work with a smile of anticipation.

"Billy, we're off now," his mother called from the bottom of the stairs. "Are you sure you'll be all right alone."

"Yes, Mum. See you later." Why do they treat me like a child? he asked himself. I'm, a teenager. What are they going to do, get a girl a year or so older than me to babysit? He thought about that one. Not a bad idea after all. "Snap out of it Bill," he said aloud. "You've got a project to finish."

"Ahem!" It sounded as though someone was clearing his throat right there in the room with him. "Good evening, Billy."

The boy twisted about in his chair. Sitting

behind him, perched on the edge of the bed, was a small, pink-faced, wrinkled man with a shiny bald head and piercing red eyes. He was wearing purple flowing robes with a hood hanging down the back which made him look for all the world like a trendy, but very short, monk.

"I said, good evening, Billy," the stranger repeated, calmly.

"What the ..." was all the youngster could manage in reply.

The short, pinkish man pulled a black leather diary from the breast pocket of his robe and scribbled a short note inside.

"Lacks manners also," he mumbled as he wrote.

"Who, or what, in the world are you?"

"You may call me Mr Thirteen," the intruder said, hopping down from the bed and holding out a tiny pink hand to the boy. "How do you do."

Too stunned to do otherwise, Billy took the little man's hand and shook it mechanically. "What do you want from me?"

"Well, Billy, it's like this," Mr Thirteen began, climbing onto the edge of the boy's desk and sitting cross-legged, nose to nose with his host. "Another guy called Bill, you'll know his stuff from school, once said — 'There are more things in heaven and earth than you ever dreamed of.' That's not it exactly, but it'll do for now."

Just what I need right now, thought Billy. A goblin misquoting Shakespeare at me.

"One of these things, or forces, is what you call superstition."

"Hey! That only works if you believe in it."

"Wrong, Billy. I'm in charge of superstition around here and I can make it work any way I like. Most of the time people who ignore my superstitions pay in small ways. Ways you'd hardly notice. You know — bad luck."

"Oh! I see. You're in charge of bad luck, are you?"

"Don't be silly, boy," snapped Thirteen, angrily. "I just said I run the superstition racket locally. That's all. You don't ever want to meet the guy who looks after luck. Not like this, anyhow."

"And what exactly do you mean by 'like this'?"

"You, my dear Billy, have got me rightly annoyed. Not only did you ignore the rituals laid down for salt spillage earlier on, but you made fun of them. Then you had the cheek to say that superstition, my superstition, is all rubbish. Now, you're going to have to pay for that."

"You don't seriously expect me to believe all this, do you?"

"Think about it, Billy. How many people do you know have had a visit from a three foot tall man with red eyes? Not that many, I'll bet. My very presence here is proof of what I say."

"It's got to be something I ate," said Billy.

"Okay, fine. Have it your way," said Mr Thirteen sliding down off Billy's desk top. "Tomorrow morning," he continued, pointing a finger at the boy's chest, "you're going to have a piece of bad luck. And that bit of bad luck is going to stay with you all day, at least. You just remember why it's happening and I'll see you tomorrow night." The little man stamped angrily across Billy's bedroom and pulled open the door. "We'll see if it was something you ate tomorrow, won't we," sneered Thirteen, storming out.

Billy jumped out of his seat and ran to the door. "Listen, I don't care ..." he was talking to thin air. He raced downstairs but there wasn't a sign of his visitor to be found. He slowly mounted the stairs, shaking his head. "Weird," he said, in a shaky voice. "Truly ... awesomely ... weird."

The next morning Billy rolled his bicycle out of the garage only to find that he had a flat tyre. "We all know how this happened," he said, picturing a short pink man holding a knife. "Real mystical piece of bad luck that is." He glanced at his wristwatch, realizing as he did so that he'd have to run if he was to catch the school bus. As he raced out of the driveway he saw the rear end of the bus disappearing into the distance and with it his chances of getting to school on time.

"Great," he muttered, as he scuffed his way along the pavement to the bus-stop to wait with the other commuters for the regular service.

He arrived into his first class, Geography, fifteen minutes after the bell. "Sorry I'm late, Sir," he said, slipping behind his desk.

Mr Ryan, the Geography teacher, grunted a dismissal of his apology. "You're project is due in this morning," he said, without lifting his eyes from the homework he was correcting for his next class.

"Yes, Sir, I've got it right here," Billy replied, pulling a large folder out of his schoolbag.

"Is it going to grow legs and walk up here by itself?" asked Rhino, mildly, drawing muffled giggles from Billy's classmates. "Bring it up here," he roared.

Billy scrambled out of his seat and walked as fast as he could, without breaking into a trot, to Mr Ryan's desk. He handed the bad-tempered teacher his project folder.

"Is this some kind of joke?"

"Joke, Sir?"

"Joke, Sir," mimicked Rhino. "Joke, boy," the teacher continued angrily. "It's a thing designed to make people laugh." He stared hard at Billy who had no idea what was going on.

Had Rhino finally flipped his trolley? wondered the boy.

"The problem is, William, that I don't have such a sense of humour, as you well know."

"I'm sorry. Sir. I just don't understand what you're talking about."

"This, boy," he said, holding out Billy's project folder. "This is what I'm talking about."

Billy stared helplessly at the pages of his folder. Every one was blank. What happened to his project? Mr Thirteen. Of course. He must have crept back into the bedroom during the night and replaced the project with blank pages. Even as the thought crossed his mind his eyes came to rest on the top page. It had a faint peanut-butter smear on one corner. He'd dropped a smudge of peanut-butter from a sandwich onto the top page of his project. And in exactly the same spot. And he hadn't been able to clean off the mark completely — just like the mark on the page in front of him. I don't like what you're thinking, he said to himself. No way can writing just disappear without trace off a page. Just like magic, he thought.

"Well?" demanded Ryan.

"I thought ..."

"What. You thought I wouldn't check your work." The teacher paused for a few seconds, staring at the boy. "See me after school. Two hours detention. Now sit down."

"But, Sir. Mr Ryan, I've got basketball practice this afternoon."

"Hard luck."

"If I don't go to practice they won't pick me for the game on Saturday."

"Isn't life tragic," said Rhino, smiling for the first time since Billy had arrived into class.

And so Billy spent two hours in detention and lost his place in the basketball squad. He brooded his way through dinner that evening and splashed and clunked his way through the washing-up afterwards. His parents cast concerned glances at one another but said nothing. He was a good kid. Everyone had bad moods once in a while. He finished the dishes and retired to his room in silence to await the reappearance of Mr Thirteen. Unable to doubt that the little man would return, after the evidence of his day's luck, the boy sat down at his desk staring through unseeing eyes at his unopened school books.

"Ahem!"

Billy whirled. As he had expected Thirteen was sitting on the edge of his bed.

"You let the air out of my tyre," Billy accused him angrily.

"Hold it, Billy boy. I admit that I caused you a little bad luck, but nothing as crude as letting your tyre down."

"You also said one piece of bad luck."

"That's right. And that's all I did. One little thing."

"Little? I was late for school, I got into detention and I've been left out of the basketball team."

"A little luck goes a long way. Especially when it's bad."

"Yeah! But that's three things."

"No, Billy. The flat tyre was carelessness. If you remember it was soft last night when you got home. You were going to fix it after you did your homework. But you forgot."

"Oh! That's right," admitted the boy. "But it's your fault I forgot. If you hadn't come along last night I would've remembered."

"Sorry, Billy. That's one down to you."

"My project? Now, you can't say you had nothing to do with that. Projects don't just disappear."

"The project was my doing," said Thirteen.

"And the basketball?"

"I did say that one piece of bad luck would stay with you. Didn't I?"

"Well it's still your fault."

"Only indirectly. Anyway, that's the way luck works."

"Now I've got to do that project again. What

about that?"

"Check the folder. I think you'll find that everything is back to normal. And I cleaned off that peanut-butter stain."

"Gee, thanks."

"And superstition?" asked Thirteen. "Do you still think it's all rubbish?"

"No," said Billy. "I'll watch my step from now on."

"And I'll be watching it also. But obviously, even someone like me can't be everywhere at once. So to be really sure that you've learned well I'm going to set you a little task for the next week."

"Aw! Come on. Haven't you done enough already. It was only a little bit of salt I spilt."

Thirteen ignored his outburst, deep in thought. "Got it," he cried, grinning at the boy. "For the next week you must avoid stepping on the cracks in the pavement. If for any reason, and I mean any reason, Billy, you should step on a crack I'm going to turn you into a frog." The little man's grin got wider and wider until it threatened to swallow his ears.

"A frog?" blurted Billy. "Gimme a break."

"I knew you weren't truly convinced. That's

why I'm setting you this test. If you fail it, you'll deserve to be a frog. If you pass you'll remember to honour my superstitions for the rest of your life." The goblin-like man reached out and placed his hand on Billy's. It was strangely cold and clammy to the touch. "Goodbye for now, Billy. I'll be seeing you."

With that Thirteen vanished, just like switching off a light. Billy looked at his hand, where the little man had touched it. There, on the back, right in the middle, stood a large wart with long black hairs growing out of it.

"That's just a reminder," said Thirteen's voice, sounding as if it came from inside his head. "But, hey! Don't worry about it, Billy boy. You'll do this standing on your head. I'll be back in a week and everything will be normal again." Then the voice chuckled evilly, causing the boy to shudder. "Or else I'll be back to pick up my frog. We can't have magical frogs hopping about the countryside, can we? I mean, what would happen if a passing princess gave you a kiss." The voice broke up in peals of uproarious laughter and faded out, like a weak radio station on a cheap transistor.

Billy sat at his desk, frightened, for several

minutes. He hadn't an idea what to do now. There was a gentle tap on the door. It opened and his mother came in.

"Why Billy, You look as if you've seen a ghost."

"Not a ghost, Mum. A goblin." It was out before he had time to think. He glanced up at his mother. She looked worried.

"A goblin? You think you saw a goblin?"

Billy had visions of the little men in their white coats coming to take him to the funny farm. Would his mother understand what had happened? She'd probably just laugh. But he had to talk about this to somebody, and at least if she thought he'd gone nuts she'd keep it to herself.

"Sit down, Mum. I've got something to tell you," he said, seriously.

His mother sat on the edge of his bed, in almost the exact spot Thirteen had occupied only minutes earlier. Then he told her the entire tale, not leaving out a thing, and as proof showed her his project folder complete with the restored project.

"If I was making this up do you think I'd have gone to the trouble of actually doing the project. You can check with Rhino ... Mr

Ryan. It's the same folder. And the project's good. I've been working on it for a couple of weeks."

"I'm sorry, Billy. I'm sure there's a rational explanation for what's happened. Maybe you only think it was the same folder. You probably fell asleep and dreamed up this Mr Thirteen. I know you're disappointed about the basketball game, but you'll get over it." She stood up. "I think you should go to bed and get some sleep. If you're still not feeling well in the morning, you don't have to go to school. Alright?"

"But, Mum. It's true. I swear."

"You get a good night's sleep and you'll see things differently in the morning. Goodnight," she said, closing his bedroom door softly behind her.

For the next few days Billy was unusually quiet. His father figured it was because of losing his place on the team for Saturday. His mother thought it better that his father kept this belief. On the day of the game Billy couldn't even bring himself to go along as a spectator, even though his parents did their best to persuade him, and all his friends would be there. After lunch his mother made a last attempt to cheer him up.

"Isn't that movie you wanted to see, Death something or other, on at the Plaza this weekend?"

"Yeah!" he replied listlessly.

"Well ... I stopped by the cinema yesterday and picked up tickets for this afternoon's show. I thought you and me could go along and then maybe on to McDonald's afterwards."

"You booked for *Death Weekend*?"

"Correct."

Billy threw his arms about his mother and hugged her. For the first time all week he looked happy. "Okay! Let's get going. We don't want to miss the opening. I read in Horror Monthly that they used two hundred gallons of fake blood shooting the first five minutes. And that's only while they run the credits. Are you coming Dad?"

"Not me. Only one of us is being sacrificed to *Death Weekend*," his father laughed, relieved to see his son coming back to his normal bouncy self.

Billy and his mother drove to the cinema in good spirits, both of them avoiding the subject of the goblin. They couldn't get parking right outside but found a car park only two streets away. As they walked towards the picture house Billy's mother could not ignore the fact that her son was bobbing about avoiding the cracks in the pavement.

"Stop that, Billy. You're making a show of us."

He didn't answer. He kept concentrating on missing the cracks.

"Billy, I'm talking to you. Walk beside me properly."

The boy stopped. His mother stopped a few paces further on.

"Mum. Whatever you may think, I was deadly serious when I told you about the goblin. Have you seen this," he asked, holding up his hairy wart for her inspection. "The goblin did this to prove his power to me and to remind me about his threat."

"It's only a wart, Billy," his mother said gently. "Lots of people get warts. Come on, we'll be late."

She turned on her heel and set off once again at a brisk pace towards the cinema. Billy bobbed along a little quicker and drew alongside her.

"Look, Billy," she said, beginning to get

annoyed with his antics. "I'll take responsibility for you stepping on the cracks." And as she said it she reached out and pushed lightly against his shoulder, throwing him off balance.

Billy stumbled and his right foot plonked down right across a crack. He teetered for a moment and then his left fell — right across yet another.

"There you are," his mother said triumphantly. "You've stepped on a crack, two cracks, and you're not a frog. Now, let's forget all about this foolishness and enjoy the rest of our day out."

Doubt about Mr Thirteen's threat seeped into his mind for the first time since the wart. It was true that he'd stepped on a crack. It was also true that he was still a boy — not a frog. He shrugged his shoulders. His mum was right. There was nothing to do now but forget about the goblin and enjoy the movie.

When they got home Billy was his normal happy self, describing to his dad in detail all the goriest scenes from *Death Weekend* and acting out several murders complete with horrible screams and a lot of leaping about.

"Are you quite finished, Bill?" his father

asked as the boy paused to catch his breath.

"Oh! no Dad. There's lots more," he said happily.

"I see. It's just that Dave from the basketball team phoned. The team won and there's a bit of a party going on over at his house. He said that they'd all like you to come over."

"When?"

"Right away. They've been celebrating since the game finished."

"Your bike still punctured?" asked his mother. He nodded. "Okay then! I'll give you a lift."

"It's all right, Dave's isn't far. I'll walk."

"Never look a gift horse in the mouth," said his mother, picking up the car keys and heading for the door.

As they drove to Dave's, Billy sat with his elbow out the window. He smiled over at his mother.

"Isn't is a lovely evening," he said.

"It's not like you to notice mundane things like the weather."

"Well, it's kinda like a weight has been lifted off my shoulders, you know? What with the worry over my goblin and the team and everything. You tend to appreciate the ordinary things after that sort of experience. It's nice to be able to just think about long sunny evenings and stuff like that."

They pulled up outside Dave's house and Billy hopped out. He walked around to the driver's side of the car, stuck his head through the open window and kissed his mum on the cheek.

"What's come over you. It's ages since you kissed me. I thought you'd grown out of that sort of thing."

"I just wanted to say thanks for being a great mum."

His mother began to drive away, leaving Billy looking fondly after her. Suddenly his attention was caught by a movement in the rear window of the car. Standing on the back seat, grinning hugely and waving at Billy was Mr Thirteen. His mother's words earlier in the day rang in his ears.

"I'll take responsibility for you stepping on the cracks."

As if the goblin could read the youngster's thoughts, Thirteen began nodding his head. Ignoring Dave, who was walking out of the house to greet him, Billy sprinted after the departing vehicle.

"Mum," he called. "Mum, stop."

But she was too far away to hear him. He waved his arms, willing her to glance in her rearview mirror. In vain. He ran back to Dave.

"Forget something?" enquired Dave.

"No time to talk, Dave," he panted. "Can you loan me your bike."

"Sure. No problem. But what's going on?"

"The bike, Dave, please."

Dave could read worry and fear in his friend's face. Without another word he hurried around the side of his house and half-wheeled, half-dragged his bike out.

"There you go, Billy. You can tell me about it later."

"Yeah! Maybe later," Billy called over his shoulder. "And thanks, Dave," he yelled, standing up on the pedals and pushing with all his strength.

He knew that his mother wasn't the fastest of drivers. There was a short-cut across a field that would save him half a mile but it was still unlikely that he could overhaul the car before home. How long before Thirteen made his move, wondered Billy. Pushing thoughts of a green warty mother out of his mind he pedalled as fast as his legs would go. It's the final burst into Paris in the Tour de France, he said to himself. Sean Kelly is only five seconds in front and tiring. Go, go. go.

He hit the final turn about ten miles an hour too fast. Suddenly the tyres lost grip and he leaned too far over and he and bike skidded off the road into a hedge. He lay for a moment, his legs tangled up in the bike. From where he lay he could see his own house. The car stood in the driveway. Maybe everything was all right.

He pulled his feet from under the bike and stood up. As he did so he saw Mr Thirteen appear out of the driveway of his home. The little man was holding one end of a dog-lead in his left hand. Behind him, on the other end of the lead, hopped a large, fat, bright green frog. The goblin and his charge ambled casually away in the opposite direction and vanished around a bend in the road.

Billy stood by the crashed bicycle, unaware of some nasty gashes he had picked up in the fall. His legs didn't seem to want to move from the spot on which he stood. He was too afraid of what he was going to find at home.

"Mum," he called, almost in a whisper. "Mum," he screamed, regaining control of his limbs and running full speed to his house. He charged to the front door and pulled out his key. In his haste it dropped to the ground. "Mum," he whispered as he regained the key and operated the lock. He pushed the door open silently. Did his dad know what was going on? What was he going to tell him? The truth? He heard voices coming from the kitchen.

"Now, drink that," his father was saying. "And from the top, tell me what happened. I couldn't make head nor tale of what you were saying when you came in."

"When I arrived home," he heard his mother's voice say, relief washing over him, "there was a goblin standing in the porch."

"A goblin," repeated his father, his voice colourless.

"Yes, and he was holding this huge, revolting frog in his arms."

"Frog," his father repeated, seemingly unable to function as more than an echo.

"And when I walked up to the door, this horrible little creature pushes the frog up towards my face."

"Face," said Billy's dad.

"Will you stop repeating every word I say."

"Sorry love. It's just that this is a bit hard to take."

"Do you want to hear it, or not?"

"Yes, of course. Go on."

"Anyway, the goblin holds up the frog and he leers at me. 'Lady, he says that you came close.' And with his free hand he holds his thumb and forefinger a fraction apart. Then he drops the frog, which he's got on a dog's lead by the way, and begins to back away from the house."

"'Just don't walk under any ladders,' he says, and strolls off down the driveway."

"Do you seriously expect me to believe this?" asks Billy's father, reasonably.

"It's all true. You can ask Billy, he's seen the goblin. He'll tell you."

"Don't bet on it," said Billy softly to himself, watching a look of mingled disbelief and pity cloud his father's face. Without a word he let himself quietly back out through the front door.

Cloudchaser

Morgan Llywelyn

Cloudchaser
Morgan Llywelyn

ichael lived in his nose. He lived in his ears, too, but mostly in his nose. He swam through an atmosphere of smells, sorting out those he recognized, wondering about the ones he did not know.

Smell was his substitute for colour. For sight.

The sea, for instance, smelled like salt and cold and dank and rotting fish, all mixed together with a high wild tingle in his nose on windy days. On days when he felt the heat of the sun on his head, the sea had a different mood and smell.

Michael's head was crowned with copper coloured hair, his mother told him. But she could not explain what copper looked like, just that it was a metal. "Reddish," she said rather doubtfully, staring at one of her copper cooking pots.

"Let me taste it," the boy urged.

He held the copper pot to his tongue. The taste was flat and slightly bitter, with an undertone of the Fairy Liquid Mammy had used to wash the pot.

My hair is that colour, Michael thought to himself, nodding his head, the smell of the dishwashing liquid lingering in his nose.

Michael was still very small when he realized there was a term for him that apparently did not apply to everyone else. He was blind, people said. Said the word with pity.

Pity smelled like dust.

"What is blind, Mammy?"

She hesitated. "It means you can't see, dear," she said in a voice gentled by having rehearsed the answer for a long time.

"What is see?"

"Looking at things with your eyes."

Michael explored his eyes with his fingers. He felt round shapes behind a fold of skin, and little stubby eyelashes. "My eyes don't work," he decided.

Mammy had a faint sob in her voice as she

replied, "Before you were born I had a sickness called rubella. It damaged your eyes."

"Oh." Michael accepted the explanation and went back to his playing. Later he would hear his father say, almost boastfully, "Michael doesn't know he's blind."

This was not true. He did know, but it meant nothing to him. He had never seen. He had never flown, either, soaring up into the clouds the way birds did in the stories Mammy read to him. He was simply sightless and flightless. He did not think of either condition as a handicap. His parents could not fly either.

He thought he would rather be able to fly than to see, if he had a choice. His earliest memory of Mammy reading was a beautiful description of clouds. "Piled up like mounds of ice cream," she had said. Michael liked to imagine himself flying through clouds of ice cream. Strawberry ice cream his favourite.

Michael's father smelled like tobacco and wool. His mother smelled like soap and something called makeup, which she said made her face pretty.

"How can you tell if your face is pretty?"

Michael wondered.

"By looking at it in the mirror."

"What's a mirror?"

"A piece of glass that reflects things in the room around you, so you can see them."

Michael considered this. "But if you can already see them with your eyes, why see them in a mirror?"

"I can't see my own face with my eyes," Mammy told him.

"I can't see mine either," Michael reminder her.

Her sharp intake of breath warned him that his words had hurt her somehow. He would have to be more careful, he thought. His blindness seemed to bother other people more than it bothered him.

He moved easily through familiar territory. He knew where all the furniture was in the house, and how many steps led down to the footpath. He could go by himself to the corner shop if Jason went with him, the big square head bobbing along near his hip. Jason was his dog, a solid shaggy dog who was described to him as black.

But black was not a colour, Daddy said. Black was an absence of colour. This puzzled

Michael. Being blind also involved an absence of colour. Yet Jason was not blind.

Michael finally decided black was the colour Jason smelled, an odour like that of wet crisps crumbled up in your hand.

Mammy had taught Michael to tell coins apart by their size and shape, and allowed him to go to the shop to buy milk and bread for her. And strawberry ice-cream.

Walking home with the ice cream, he secretly pretended he was carrying clouds in a sack.

When Michael was old enough he went to school. In school he learned to read the written language of the blind, called Braille, by using his fingertips. The whole world opened up to him. He would no longer have to ask Mammy to read to him. He could read for himself. There were special books for people who could not see and he read every one he could get. At first he was in a class with other blind children, and a teacher who knew how to teach them. He liked school, but he did not like being set apart. He did not like the tone of voice people sometimes used when they were talking about him, as if he was not there. He did not like the way strangers sometimes smelled when they met him, a fearful smell, stale and sour.

When he first went to school and met the other blind children, they did not talk about being blind. Children who had feet did not talk about having feet. They talked about the things all children talked about, they teased each other and laughed a lot and were cruel and kind.

Michael's first teacher was called Mrs Kearney. One day he asked her, "Did you ever fly?"

"In an airplane, you mean? I have."

"Did the airplane have windows? Did you look outside and see the clouds?"

"I did." Her voice had a smile in it. Michael liked voices with smiles in them.

"What are clouds like, Mrs Kearney?"

She thought for a moment. "Like feathers," she said. "They float in the air like masses and masses of feathers."

That night Michael fiddled with his down comforter until he pulled a little feather loose. He smelled it, he worked it with his fingers until he knew all there was to learn about the feather.

Clouds were like feathers and ice cream.

His mind stretched, trying to understand clouds.

A year passed, then another, and another. Michael's legs grew longer. Jason's head only came to his knee now. He had many friends, some who could see and some who could not. Jason knew who Michael's friends were and always wagged his tail when one of them called in. Michael felt the thick tail beating a welcome against his own leg. Jason stood close to Michael when anyone else was nearby. Jason thought he was supposed to protect Michael.

Michael felt almost grown. He did not think he needed Jason to protect him, but he always patted Jason's head and said, "Good dog," to thank him.

In school, Michael was learning maths and geography and Irish. In his classroom was a globe of the world, with raised areas to show the continents. Michael ran his fingers over the globe, feeling Europe and Africa and North America. He wondered if God ever ran His fingers over the spines of the mountains, feeling them.

Perhaps clouds were God's fingers, drifting across the globe, feeling the land beneath.

Michael had a hungry mind and he filled it with learning.

"The lad's a scholar," The Dad said. He was The Dad now, not Daddy, because Michael was older, almost grown. But Mammy was still Mammy and still worried about Michael. There was a certain tone in her voice that was not there when she spoke to the other children, to Patrick or Eileen or Liam.

"Don't worry about me," Michael wanted to say to her. "I shall be all right." He was certain of it. He would finish growing up, and have a job, and a wife, and children who smelled at first like milk and talcum.

He was almost certain of it. Except sometimes. Sometimes he worried. He was old enough to know that life was not easy, and jobs were not easy to find. A man who could not see could not do every job.

He could not be an airline pilot.

Michael had once dreamed of being a pilot and flying in the clouds. But at some stage he had folded up that dream and laid it away in a secret place inside himself.

His teachers told him many things unsighted people could do. There were machines and computers and places in industry; there was teaching, there were businesses one could learn. Michael would not have to depend on charity. He would make his own money, he was determined, and be like everyone else. He *was* like everyone else.

Except he had never seen clouds.

His fingers flew over his books, learning new words for clouds. Towering, scudding, lowering, billowing ... His lips shaped the words. Images roiled through his mind. Yet he had never smelled clouds, never heard clouds, never touched clouds. He could not make them seem real, as the metal curve of a car bonnet was real because he could run his hands over it.

Perhaps, Michael thought, there are no clouds. Perhaps it's just a story someone made up. How would I know?

The thought frightened him. Suddenly the world seemed threatening. How much of it was real? How much of it could he believe?

When Michael was twelve years old, his family went on holiday to Kerry. Mammy's mother came from Kerry, though she had been dead a long time. But Mammy wanted to see the house where she was born, and the cemetery where she was buried, and talk to people who remembered. So they packed clothes and put Jason and petrol into the car, and drove for a long time. Michael liked the long drive. He liked the sense of motion, and the way the smells of the country changed as they moved along. He kept the window rolled down so he could smell them, and his head and Jason's poked out together, sniffing the air.

They smelled apple trees and cows and mud and rain and cars and wind and roast chicken and fresh chippings. They stopped for tea in a town that smelled nothing like the city, and when they drove on again the air was different, lighter, sweeter.

Michael and Jason drank it with their noses.

They spent the night in a bed-and-breakfast that smelled like furniture polish and bacon. The linen on Michael's bed was worn very soft, but his pillow was hard and he could not find the right place for his head. When he awoke the strangeness of the room was like a quivering in the air around him. Mammy came in and walked with him to the room where they ate breakfast, and told him in a low voice where the food was on his plate, and where his glass was placed.

Michael wondered if other people were looking at him. He hid in the darkness behind his eyes, feeling shy.

"Today we'll drive over Conor Pass," The Dad announced. "The sun's shining, it should be beautiful."

Beautiful was not a word that meant anything to Michael. Like clouds, it had no smell or taste. But he smiled anyway, and Mammy ruffled his coppery hair with her hand.

They drove slowly, and Michael could feel that the car was climbing. There was a pressure in his ears. "Swallow," The Dad said. "Swallow hard."

When Michael swallowed hard the pressure went away.

The car climbed up and up, turning and turning. It began to go very slowly. The Dad shifted the gears down and down again. The car made a grunting noise each time.

"The clouds are so thick ... " Mammy said in an anxious voice. "Should we go back? It doesn't look safe to try and go on in this."

"There's no place to turn around just yet,"

The Dad said. His voice was tense, too, but Michael did not notice.

Mammy had said the clouds were thick, and a new smell was coming in the window.

Moisture lay on Michael's face with a weight he could feel.

"What clouds?" he said eagerly.

"All around us," Mammy replied. "We've driven up into them."

"Oh, please stop!"

"Don't be frightened, lad," The Dad said. "I can drive ..."

"I'm not frightened, I just want to feel the clouds! Please stop. Let me taste them!" Michael's voice rose, skittering higher and higher in his eagerness. He squirmed in his seat and Jason whined in sympathy.

"Right, so. As soon as I can," The Dad promised. But they drove on, so slowly Michael wanted to beat on the seat with his fists. Then at last he felt the car shudder to a stop. "This is the lookout." The Dad said.

Michael fumbled for the door handle. Mammy caught his shoulder. "Don't get out, you'll just step off into space," she said. She sounded frightened.

But Michael was not frightened. He was

among clouds. *Among clouds*! He had to get out. "Jason needs out," he insisted.

The Dad laughed. "I'll take you both," he said. "Hold on."

Michael heard the faint screech of the hand brake being lifted, then a click as The Dad unfastened his seat belt. The fabric made a rasping sound as he slid out. The door opened, closed. Michael's door opened and The Dad reached in, taking Michael's hand.

"You sit there," he said to Mammy. "It's safe."

Mammy was breathing fast with a little catch in her throat, but for once Michael could not worry about her feelings. He could only think of the clouds, waiting.

Jason leaped from the car in a flurry of fur and feet. Michael got out more slowly, letting his father's hand guide him. They walked a few steps together, then stopped.

"Now," said The Dad. "The clouds are sitting so low on the mountain that we're right in the middle of them. They're grey and ..."

But Michael was not listening to his father's description of clouds. He did not need to know they were grey; grey had no meaning. Their smell was their colour, and their smell was that of furze and heather and damp sheep, of wiry grass and flinty stone and a thick, sweet moisture that seeped into Michael's nose and throat.

Clouds were real. They had weight against his skin and left tiny beads of moisture. They carried exotic scents from far away; these clouds had crossed the Atlantic, forming and forming again, bringing with them memories of beaches and islands and distant lands.

The clouds told Michael's nose about the world beyond, and the dark wild sea.

Among the clouds, Michael did not need to see. He could smell and taste and feel. He could feel the feathery touches of the clouds upon his face, and the swirling of the air around him. He breathed in clouds. He tasted clouds. He lost himself in clouds.

From far away, he heard The Dad's voice. "We have to go now, so." A hand shook Michael by the shoulder, tugging at him.

With a great effort, Michael drew back from the clouds and let himself be led to the car. But even after he was in his seat again he pressed against the locked door, leaning out, toward the clouds.

The road turned and turned and dropped, and the clouds were left behind. But Michael was filled with them.

When they reached Dingle they stopped for a meal and to ask directions. Then they drove out a bumpy little road that seemed to go forever, while Mammy talked about her grandparents and her own childhood, and The Dad kept the car on the road and tried not to hit a sheep.

When the car stopped this time, there was a happy lilt in Mammy's voice. "I know this cottage!" she cried. She jumped out of the car without waiting for The Dad to open for her as she usually did. Michael heard her feet running like a young girl's feet, and then the door of a house opened and there were calls and greeting.

Mr McGillicuddy remembered Mammy as a little girl, when she used to visit Kerry in the summer, and Mrs McGillicuddy liked boys and made very good scones with cheese in them. Michael curled up on a couch and listened to the adults talk, from time to time slipping a bit of scone to Jason, who sat at his feet.

"You used to play the fiddle for us," Mammy recalled at some stage, and the old man laughed. "I did for a fact. But it's been donkey's years, the arthritis is in the fingers now."

"Do you still have the fiddle?"

"It's around here someplace."

Michael, still thinking of the clouds in the pass, was not paying much attention until he heard the voice of the violin. The sound was wild and strange and familiar at the same time. It was like the wind blowing through the pass; it was like the sea beating on the rocks.

He got off the couch and made his way to the old man's side guided by the sound of the music.

"Do you play, lad?"

"I've never tried. But I like music." Michael heard his mother murmuring some apology for his blindness, but the old man had already cupped the boy's fingers around the neck of the fiddle and tucked the instrument beneath his chin. He put the bow in Michael's other hand, and his own rough, calloused hand over it. Then he began to play. The sound went through Michael's bones.

They spent three weeks in Kerry and Michael spent every day with Mr McGillicuddy. By the time the holiday was over he could play the fiddle without the old man's hands guiding his, and without the instrument screeching like a cat hit by a lorry. When they were ready to return home, Mr McGillicuddy gave the fiddle to Michael.

"We couldn't possibly," Mammy protested.

"It's little use to me now, I won't play it again. And the lad has a grand touch on it. Take it so, make us both happy."

All the way home, Michael kept the fiddle pressed to his chest. The smell of the wood and the varnish and the strings and the resin mingled in his head with the memory of clouds. He lifted the bow. Jason pressed his head against Michael's knee and whined softly, his tail thumping as the boy began to play.

"What is that tune?" Mammy asked. "I've never heard it before."

"Just something in my head." Michael's fingers sought among the strings, pressing and releasing. Slowly at first, then more surely, he made the fiddle recall the clouds. With sound he described the achingly sweet fragrance of heather and the softness of damp air. He found chords to billow and blow. He played a sea breeze and then a rumble of thunder. He drew the clouds out of himself, into the violin, and the violin sang them aloud.

When the music died Mammy said softly, "That was beautiful." And Michael knew what she meant. Beautiful had meaning for him now.

"Do you think you could play it again?" The Dad asked. There was a tone in his voice Michael was hearing for the first, but not the last, time. Respect.

"I could," Michael said.

The music was part of him as the clouds were part of him. When he thought about it, he could make music describe so many things he knew, experiences of smell and touch and taste. Shaggy Jason lumbering along at his side; hot soup bubbling in the pot. He could even play the loneliness he sometimes felt in the darkness behind his eyes.

Without the distraction of sight, Michael had learned through his other senses. In the privacy of his blindness he had also learned to know himself. Now everything that was in him was waiting to come out in the music.

In the back seat of the car headed for home, Michael hugged the violin to his chest and dreamed of captured clouds.

The Footpath

Hugh O'Neill

The Footpath
Hugh O'Neill

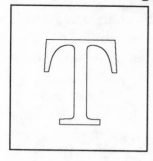

These were the days all the lads in our gang had been looking forward to: freedom, the summer holidays from school, the things we would be doing, cowboys and Indians across Lynch's fields and jail-breaking up the line by the old canal. Then there was hunting in the old mysterious woods beside our house, with all its secret passages and spooky hideouts and the big haunted house right in the middle. Nobody dared go in there alone, except the bravest lads.

I was hoping to get a job this summer, gathering spuds in Newmills or maybe picking strawberries in Loughall, where all the big farmers are. My dad says our ancestors used to own all those lands before they were robbed and given to "the planters," people loyal to the English throne. But my mum says that was hundreds of years ago, and isn't it better to get a few bob out of them now when you get the chance. Dad says he doesn't want any of his children to be used as slave labour by anyone, and those days are coming to an end in this country!

All I know is that if I have two pounds and ten shillings saved I'll be able to buy the big red fishing rod in McGlinchey's shop window, and then go down to "the point" on the river Blackwater. If old Barney can catch fish with a sally-wobble stick, a piece of fishing line, a whiskey-bottle cork as a float and a fishing hook, then I can catch hundreds of them with my new rod. Barney says it's the smell of the whiskey that attracts the fish, but I don't believe that! I'm lying here now in the sun, daydreaming about the fish I'll catch—trout, pike and my favourites, eels. We'll build a fire and cook them on our old frying pan, roast a few spuds in the fire and camp out by the river with all the lads.

But it's really the job I want. Dad says it will help me stand up in the world. "Meeting the stranger will teach you," he says.

We are into the second week of our summer holidays and all the lads in the gang are here in our back garden. Most of them are bored and discussing what to do for the day. Kevin Croner suggests we go to the washing bay, the beach at Lough Neagh. It's only a three-and-a-half mile walk, and if we are lucky we may get a lift.

Kevin is small and strongly built, with dark curly hair, and is the streetwise joker in our gang. My mum says he always has the last answer.

Eamonn says he's not walking three and a half miles to swim again because by the time you walk down and get a swim you're too tired to walk home, which is exactly what happened to us last week! My mum says that Eamonn, who is small, fair-haired and, everybody says, cheeky, is "a likeable lad, for all that." Patsy Sweeney, nick-named Buddy Holly because he wears glasses and uses Brylcreem, says it would be alright, only last week some of the Annaghmore boys hid his jeans while he was swimming and he had to walk home wearing his underpants. His mum went stone mad when he arrived home. Kevin says if he gets any of the Annaghmore boys he will burst them.

Shay says maybe we should ask Patrick MacCafferty to give us a lift, since he goes down to collect turf in the moss beside the washing bay. But it's already too late for that since he left hours ago.

Fergal is the leader of our gang. He is also the oldest and he's taller and better-built than most of us, with a short-back-and-sides haircut just like a soldier. Nobody can catch him when he goes on a solo run and he can kick a point over the bar from the fifty yard line. We all say he will be playing for the Tyrone minors next year. Nobody messes with Fergal and usually what Fergal says goes. He lets us all have our speak, sits back, takes it all in and, when everybody is in the middle of disagreement, he steps in with the best plan. As usual we agree with it and follow him. Fergal always has a book in his pocket and reads at least one a week, and sometimes two. He is much given to pointing out various facts to us from his current reading.

Fergal has warned us not to tell anyone about our secret log cabin in the woods. We built it ourselves from old bits and pieces we collected. We've even fitted an old stove that we found in Annagher dump. When it's lit up the heat from it would put you out of the house. We hide there when we mitch from school. In fact, Fergal spends half his school days there. He doesn't like school that much. Brain washing, he calls it. He keeps his reading books hidden in the cabin in an old box he made from a tea chest. He waterproofed it with red paint he got from the local football club, after he painted their new hall for them. Fergal got most of his books as gifts from his grandad and old Tim Donnagher. There are even some of Master O'Neill's books in there. He encourages us to read them, frequently saying that the right kind of books are the key to knowledge.

So there we all were lying about the garden, drinking lemonade which my mum has brought out to us. Nothing to trouble us except the odd wasp buzzing around. My dad went past with his trousers rolled up to his knees and a white hanky with a knot tied at each corner on his head, and the sweat lashing off him. "Is there no work yous could be doing," he shouted at us good-humouredly. Everybody likes my dad, says he's very funny, and would always give you a lift in his car. And, says Fergal, he takes no guff from anyone.

We heard steps running down our street, steps filled with an urgency which brings us to our feet. My sister Rita was shouting, "Mammy, Mammy, Nell Connors has been knocked down by a car." Rita was pointing up the road and we all headed up there. We saw the car stopped and the driver out comforting Nell. Her leg seemed to be at right angles to her body. Now all the women in the neighbourhood were out and the driver started explaining that it's not his fault, that there should be a footpath on the road, why isn't there a footpath on the road? he asked. Sheilagh, Nell's mother, pushed past everyone and Mr Devlin told her he's phoned for an ambulance. Someone else said there was no point in calling the police since they'd take ages to arrive and laugh when they got there. Nell was pale but she wasn't crying, which surprised all the lads. If it was one of us we would be crying, for sure. Sheilagh was talking to Nell, and was relieved that it wasn't more serious, but still cross that it happened in the first place. She turned to the driver who was standing by his car looking very shook-up.

"What in hell's blazes were you doing?" she demanded in a shaky voice. "Could you not look where you were going?"

"Aw missus! It wasn't my fault. I met one of those big trucks that's drawing gravel to the new motorway. He must have been doing at least 60. He wouldn't slow down or pull in and next thing I seen was the young girl. I braked and skidded into her I'm sorry missus, but only I've got good brakes on the car she would have been killed. There should be a footpath on this road anyway, it's a busy road. Where I live in Moygashel we've got a footpath."

Up to this last statement Sheilagh had been nodding her head and listening to him. Now she raised her eyes to heaven as though asking for patience. No messages being received from there, she looked the driver straight in the eye. "It's sure there's a footpath in Moygashel," she stated plainly, "isn't that where all the privileged Loyalists live? "Sure you have footpaths. And no doubt you have streetlights too, and lollipop men on every crossroads, and no pot-holes either, is there?"

The driver swallowed hard and started explaining again about the lack of a footpath being the cause of the accident, but Sheilagh hadn't finished yet. And now she was joined by Fergal in support.

"There's no footpath here because this is a Nationalist area," he said, calmly enough. "But we've had enough now of being treated as second-class citizens, of being put through every hardship and being ignored by those bigots and bullies in power in Stormont Castle." All of us were still talking when the ambulance arrived with its blue light flashing and siren blaring. Nell was helped into it and taken to Dungannon hospital.

"She'll be alright now," said my mum to Sheilagh. "Could have been worse."

Sheilagh was grim-faced. "We're going to have to do something, before some child is killed," she said to my mum. No-one was sure what could be done, since, as one woman pointed out, we were all nationalist families, born in the wrong place at the wrong time, and they just wouldn't listen to us.

"Well," said Sheilagh looking around at

everyone, "we'll just have to have a public protest then."

Fergal immediately said that all of us would help, but a voice from the back of the crowd said, "I don't agree at all. I'm going to be gathering spuds so as I can get some money for myself." We stared at Martin Mooney, one of the Annaghmore lads, well-known for his meanness and selfishness. As we continued to stare at him, his face grew red and he said defiantly: "She should have watched where she was going, she needs glasses that girl. Anyway, I'm staying out of trouble, so I'm staying away from yous Lower Gortagonis boys, with your talk of Connolly and Wolfe Tone and Tom Barry, and singing songs about Tom Williams and him hung in gaol and all. My mum says all those people were trouble makers."

Fergal walked up to him and said in a voice just loud enough for everyone to hear that he should go home to his room and sit and admire all his great soccer stars posted on the wall and put on one of his pop music records. "And smoke one of your da's butts while you're there" he said, "it's probably the bravest thing you'll do in your life." Everyone laughed, and Mooney moved away, walking slowly towards his home.

Drawn by the sound of my mum's voice, we all drifted over to where the women were grouped. "We've put up with being treated as second class citizens in our own country now for over fifty years," she was saying to the women gathered around. "You go to any one of the Loyalists areas around here and you'll find they've got good roads and street lighting, good houses and they've all got jobs for themselves too. I don't blame our people leaving the country; all they can hope for here are the leftovers."

Mum and Dad always talked like that at home, but this sort of thing was never aired in public, and I was very surprised to hear my mother now. Before, I'd never taken much notice of such talk as I'd always had more important things to be daydreaming about, like playing and hunting and how to get a job so that I could buy a fishing rod. Now I listened with the rest of the lads as Fergal explained what the women were talking about and it was the first time any of us had heard this sort of talk, in public anyway. And, it was *our mothers* who were talking!

"Let's block the road and demand action from the council." shouted Eileen Lynch. "Let's get everybody out, women, children and there's enough men about this area unemployed—get them all out!" Well, all the women agreed, and Fergal asked us if we were going to support them. All our hands shot up in agreement. It was decided that the men should stay off the protest, since their inclusion would give the B-Specials good reason to baton us all. Fergal pointed out that we weren't "men" and that therefore we could be included. At this stage we were all worried that we were going to be told to stay at home and so miss the action.

"Our Fionnuala is trying to get a job in the Civil Service, and if our family is in the paper the Special Branch will read it and she won't get the job," said Mrs Deane.

"Look, she won't get the job anyway." said Annie Burns loudly, "where do you think you are? In a normal country?" She added in a softer tone: "Would you go and wise up with yourself; she won't get the job because she doesn't kick with the right foot!"

Sheilagh brought the crowd of us to order,

and gave us a plan of action for the following Saturday. Recognising Fergal as the lads' leader, she asked him if he could get some placards ready, and cautioned him to make sure the words were spelt correctly. "We don't want those powerfull people up there laughing at us."

All the plans we had been making for the summer just a couple of hours earlier were now diverted to this new cause. We collected wood, paint and strong sticks and brought them to the log cabin in the woods, where we all worked to make placards. We painted them black and wrote the slogans in white. By Friday afternoon we had produced a great crop.

THE PEOPLE WANT
A FOOTPATH
AND STREET LIGHTING
NOW!

**FOOTPATH NOW
BEFORE NEXT PERSON
IS KILLED!**

**Civil Rights
for
EVERYONE!**

**AN END TO
DISCRIMINATION
NOW!**

We started moving everything out of the cabin and back to my house, ready for the next day. On the way we met some of the Annaghmore lads at Tessie's Crossroads. "Are you coming with us tomorrow?" asked Fergal.

"Not us!" retorted to red-faced Mooney. "Yous will all end up in trouble and the police will baton yous off the road."

As one voice we roared at them "Mé Féiners!" and Fergal reminded them that they knew where we'd be if they changed their minds, as we'd need all the support we could get. "The police don't mind us protesting as long as we do it alone!" he muttered. As with a lot of Fergal's sayings you have to think about them for a while and then they make sense. "James Connolly without the moustache" we often slagged him

Saturday dawned, blazing hot, a great day for swimming or fishing, or even a stroll across Lynch's fields with Bruno, our dog. Maybe we could have raised a hare or a fox. But we'd more important things to do today.

Around dinnertime the lads started to gather at our house. We left Dad to do the dishes and clearing away.

"Lucky is the woman who caught me," he joked as we left, but I think he was disappointed at being left out of the protest. His parting shot followed us, "Countess Markovitch" he laughed, referring to Sheilagh, "will be waiting on her stormtroopers, so you'd better hurry." When we arrived, Sheilagh was talking tactics with all the Lower Gortagonis women who had brought prams, babies and toddlers all dressed up in their brightest and best summer clothes. Kevin Croner remarks that he's dressed up too, and points at a pair of black, steel-tipped boots, several sizes too big for him, on his feet.

Fergal started to hand around placards, making sure that they were well spaced throughout the crowd for maximum impact.

Sheilagh, looking at them, said, "great bit of work, lads."

We started walking in a big circle and it wasn't long before there was a huge traffic jam with cars, lorries, vans, tractors and trailers with cows in the back of them, horns beeping, cows mooing, and confusion everywhere. Owners started to leave their cars to see what was up, and some of them, especially the farmers, started to get angry, telling Sheilagh they needed to milk their cows. Sheilagh retorted that in that case they'd better find someone who could meet our demands for a new footpath and lighting!

"We are staying here until we get some answers, however long it takes," she announced. As more and more traffic piled up, some drivers attempted to turn around and go back, adding to the chaos.

Sheilagh and Fergal went around to all the cars and explained what the protest was about, and by the time they were finished most drivers were supporting us because they, too, had young children who might be using the road.

Suddenly a roar went up, "Here comes the cops" and a long skinny sergeant, with flat cap and two big ears, pushed his way towards Sheilagh. As is the way in these parts, he was instantly named Bin-lid. He was followed by three others who looked more like the Keystone cops than anything else.

Telling Sheilagh that we couldn't block the Queen's Highway was his first mistake.

"Don't call me Madam, my boy, and the Queen has no highways in Tyrone," Sheilagh replied sharply. "We're not moving until our demands are met. We want a footpath here and we want street lights from Coalisland to Annaghmore." Ignoring Bin-lid's threat to call in back-up manpower and equipment, Sheilagh ordered him to get onto his bosses "in the Council, in Stormont, or Westminster if need be. All we want is a footpath and street lighting, not a third world war!"

Even as I was walking backwards and forwards, I was thinking that this was not the sort of situation we were taught to deal with in school. Real-life situations, and the reality of our everyday lives, didn't figure in our school lessons. We weren't taught how to speak up for ourselves when we were right and being treated unjustly, or how the powerful always tried to bully the minority. We were really ill-informed, divided and weak, just the situation, Fergal says, which keeps the powerful in power.

Taking a good slow look around him, Bin-lid told Sheilagh he would contact his bosses to see what they had to say. We were surprised at this response, and delighted when he returned to say that the Council would be starting work on Monday morning at eight o'clock.

"Now you women should all go home and cook your husband's dinner and clean up the house. That's what women should be doing and not out in mobs on the road like this." Sheilagh asked if this was a guaranteed promise from the Council and, despite advice from people in the crowd that Bin-lid couldn't be trusted, she said alright, we'll take your word and expect to see work start on Monday morning. During all this time the other police were taking names and one of them was up on the roof of his Landrover taking photographs.

"Congratulations everyone!" said Fergal. "You have all been added to the British files up in Stormont. We should be honoured." Bin-lid glared at him and Fergal smiled back. "The natives are getting very restless, sir," he remarked.

We were all waiting for Monday to see whether the Council kept its word, and whether the papers reported the protest. My dad came in with the papers and remarked that there was no sign of the workmen, nor was there any report in the papers. "They won't report it," he said, "because it could start the whole country off protesting, and I don't believe they'll start work on the path today or any other day."

Sheilagh and my mum called a meeting a couple of nights later when it became obvious that no work was going to begin. Fergal urged that we should all protest again, start earlier, have more people and demand someone out from the Council to deal with us. Everyone agreed and the plan was again drawn up. "Tell everyone! Spread the word! Get the message out!" Fergal was telling everyone, and to us he said "no lying in bed, you lot!"

Saturday came around again, with blazing sunshine.

"It's a pity Wolfe Tone didn't get this type of weather when he was making his landing," said my father, digging into his cornflakes. "There would be no need for protesting now had he been successful." My dad has a knack of relating things that happened hundreds of years ago to things that are happening now.

"We would be fighting to put the French

out," Mum replied, sparking off a major debate on the subject. I used the excuse to rush off to the protest.

Fergal reckoned there'd be a good crowd that day with groups of lads coming from Brackaville, Annagher Hill and Derrytresk— lads we would normally only see at a football match. This was going to be a real change, working with them instead of competing against them

Women, children prams and babies started to appear from all directions, dressed in their summer clothes. "They must be expecting their pictures to be taken," Kevin remarked, as he tightened the lace on his steel-tipped boots and kicked an electric pole as if to test them out. Then someone shouted "Hold on, here comes Father McKeever." He was the local priest and he was driving a black Ford Prefect, chugging along at 20 miles an hour.

"No rush on him," Kevin said, and indeed, the good Father, to save time perhaps, ignored the stop signs at the crossroads, and drove straight on. It was Kevin's theory that he'd never had an accident because he runs the car on holy water. Sure enough Father McKeever   sailed   through,   looking

everywhere except in front of him. He saw
nothing odd in the group on the roadside at
all. Or if he did, he wasn't letting on.

There was twice the crowd now as the
previous Saturday. Even Martin Mooney and
his friends watched from a safe distance,
despite the jeering from some of the lads.

We had no sooner started walking around
than a whole convoy of lorries, heading
further north, arrived on the scene. They
were the same kind that had caused the
accident in the first place. The drivers
hopped out and demanded to get past. "Are
yous serious?" Sheilagh asked one of them.
"The speed yous drive up and down this road,
you have no thought whatsoever for anyone
living here!" Now the insults started flying
from the women on the protest towards the
drivers, and they made a hasty retreat back
to the lorries. "Everything is going just
according to plan," smiled Sheilagh at
everyone.

The confusion was worse that the previous
Saturday, with cars, lorries, vans, trucks and
tractors beeping horns and drivers shouting
at us. " A carnival of reaction," Fergal called
it. Some of the more enthusiastic protesters

wanted to let the air out of the tyres but Fergal put a stop to the idea at once.

"That would be an act of vandalism against our own people," he said. Old Joseph, out of his bed for the first time in a year, pointed out that our only target must be the people in power and those who did their dirty work. The idea dropped. Joseph had taken part in every national liberation struggle in Ireland since 1916, was in gaol in the 30s and 40s and badly wounded while on the run in the 50s campaign. His health was never the same since, but here he was now, full of life and like a spring lamb.

I heard someone shouting that Bin-lid had arrived, bringing with him what looked like every policeman in Tyrone. There were ten Land Rovers and a couple of paddy-wagons. The police were dressed in long, black coats, black crash-helmets with clear plastic visors covering their faces, and every one of them carried a baton and shield, while some also had guns. "Expected this," said Old Joseph, "they can't resist cracking nuts with sledgehammers, those buggars." Fergal shouted out: "Everyone be careful now."

Happy in the knowledge that he had

enough of his henchmen there to back him up, Bin-lid pushed his way towards Sheilagh and started shouting at her to move, to go home NOW or we would all be dragged to a paddy wagon and down to the Crumlin Road gaol. Kevin muttered that the policemen dressed in the ridiculous get-up only to scare people and make them retreat in fear, but they'd fail today because the people knew they were right.

Sheilagh folded her arms and stood in front of Bin-lid. The crowd fell silent. Sheilagh looked as though a bit of hand-to-hand combat might be OK, and Bin-lid took a couple of steps back from her blazing eyes. The silence grew longer, Bin-lid looked around and realised there was a much larger crowd here than last week, and it could get very nasty if he had to baton-charge and make arrests, what with the children and the babies in prams. He comforted himself that all the laws were in place, if he chose to take this action. But then he caught sight of a man wielding a camera, and another talking frantically into a tape recorder. Then he squinted his eyes, he could see it had BBC printed on the side. "Well?" said Sheilagh, "what have to say for yourself and your promises?"

"We got mucked up on the dates, Missus—actually it's this Monday the work will start."

"Damn you and your lies, we're not moving until we get someone up here who is in charge."

"Look missus, I can move my men in and arrest every one of this mob, and certain people are going to get hurt for sure," said Bin-lid, looking over at Fergal in anticipation of what he was going to do to teach him a few lessons when he got him into the police station.

Complete with riot gear, the police started to move through the crowd, deliberately pushing the women out of their way. But these women had been pushed around too often, and chose today to stand their ground. The photographer was rushing around in a frenzy, getting all the angles he could.

Very quietly, a voice in the crowd started to sing a Black civil-rights song, and immediately it was taken up by the whole crowd and bellowed at the police.

**We shall not
we shall not,
we shall not be moved ...**

The sound swelled up as more and more
people joined in, even the Mé Féiners sitting
on the wall down the road. Now we were all
punctuating the song with clenched fist
salutes. Bin-lid returned from his car-radio
and said that "someone" would be here soon,
and we had to get this mob off the road to let
the traffic through.

**No! No! No! No! No!
We won't go
No! No! we won't go!**

rose into the air as the crowd began to chant.
Bin-lid and his policemen looked lost and
bewildered—why were these women not
frightened of the policemen in riot gear? He
had very set ideas about what women should
be doing. They should be at home, cleaning
and cooking and washing, and their presence
here today, singing at him, upset his
understanding of the proper order of life. The

chanting grew louder and he suddenly gave the order to his men to move back "until the man in charge of the roads in this area comes out."

Morale was very high now, and everyone was in good humour. The women were in complete control of a scene which looked like a mini-battlefield. Old Joseph stood back, puffing his pipe, smiling. "Ah, the people are awakening from their slumber," he said to Fergal, who was standing at his side.

"Here comes Bin-lid," shouted Kevin.

Sure enough, he was trudging towards us accompanied by a small, chubby man, wearing a dark pinstriped suit and a black bowler hat, carrying a briefcase. As they drew closer, we noted, silently, the strong smell of aftershave from him, and saw that his face bore and uncanny resemblance to a bulldog.

I had only seen pictures of men like this on the twelfth of July, marching up and down the streets and making speeches saying that Nationalists must not be trusted and must be kept in their place. Now here was a real live one, except that he was not wearing his sash today.

"Which one of you is in charge here?" asked Bull-Dog, full of his own importance. Bin-lid pointed out Sheilagh and he turned towards her. "Are you spokesman for this mob?"

"We," said Sheilagh, in her nicest voice, "are not a mob, and I am spokeswoman for the group of people around you, yes." Taken aback by Sheilagh's words, Bulldog adopted a more conciliatory tone of voice, as he explained, in the sort of voice normally used with very small children, that the provision of a footpath and street lights in our district came very, very low on the Council's list of priorities. The Council had a lot more important things to be doing with its money, really, he offered to Sheilagh.

Sheilagh stood silent, and, taking this as her agreement that he had offered a reasonable excuse, Bull-dog started to move back to his car. The sound of Sheilagh in full, magnificent voice halted him abruptly. "Mister," she roared, bringing her face to within two inches of his, "you'd be well advised to put our footpath and lighting right to the top of your list of priorities, and start this work next Monday morning, because we're not moving from here till you do."

On cue, the whole crowd set up the chant:

No! No! We won't go!
No! No! We won't go!

Our Headmaster would have been proud of all the lads. He had been trying to get us all to join the school choir for years, without luck. We all used the excuse that we could not sing. Yet, here we were, singing at the top of our voices, not a note out of place!

Sheilagh now pressed a sheet of paper into Bulldog's hands, with the word

Agreement

written on top in big, black letters. He surveyed the scene around him, the protesters, the placards, the prams, the determination on every face; behind them, drawn up in riot formation, were the police, batons at the ready, dogs snarling, paddy-wagons with doors swinging open hungrily; then he caught sight of the photographer and reporter, still moving efficiently about the crowd.

Something like a feeling of panic set in. He

had a round of golf to get in this afternoon with the local judge. The lower classes were truly an awful breed. How would they ever keep power if people like these really thought they could take on the might of the Empire, just because they wanted street lighting. If only they would stop that chanting he could think up a credible excuse and make his escape.

But the mob had circled around him as they chanted, so he just had to stand there, trying to avoid Sheilagh's eyes as she smiled nicely at him.

"It's up to yourself, really," she said, signalling to the crowd to be silent. "We will stay here, on a peaceful protest, as long as it takes you and your friends up there to understand that we are entitled to a footpath and good lighting around here."

As the prospect of a round of golf with the judge faded, Bulldog suddenly took out a pen and started to write on the sheet of paper. Sheilagh, at his elbow, dictated the terms, with a smile playing around her mouth. The crowd stayed completely silent until she read out the agreement. Work would start the following Monday, and Bulldog had signed his name to that. As he struggled back to his car, red-faced and sweating, the crowd released its tension and went mad with joy, singing and dancing all round the streets. A lot of the drivers left their cars and lorries and joined in.

It was a great feeling to have been part of the whole thing. I felt tears in my eyes, and my throat felt tight. Looking around, I saw all the lads feeling the importance of the day too. Fergal came over to where I was standing with Old Joseph.

"We've won this battle OK," he said to us, "but I fear we've a long war ahead of us yet."

The Tale of the Missing Mouse

Dolores Walshe

The Tail of the Missing Mouse
Dolores Walshe

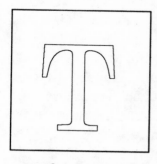

he day my cousin Egbert came from Australia to visit us was the worst day of my life. Do you know why? Because three really horrible things happened.

Number one, I was accused of STEALING. Can you beat that!

Number two, my BEST FRIEND became my WORST ENEMY.

Number three, my best and only animal friend was KIDNAPPED.

AND IT WAS ALL EGBERT'S FAULT.

I'll bet all your horrible things never happened on the same day like that.

And this is the way it happened.

My Mom, Dad, Joey my little brother and I went to the airport to collect Egbert. But first I'd better tell you who I am. My name's Sam, short for Samantha, but everybody calls me Sam because I'm a tomboy. I'm twelve years old and I love snow, swimming, chips, ice-cream, hamburgers, sweets, cake, animals, especially mice, Superman, Supergran and Ghostbusters. I hate school, teachers, all vegetables, especially cauliflower and cabbage, dresses, especially the fancy, frilly kind that make you look like a Christmas decoration, and boys, except my kid brother Joey who's quite lovable, although I know he won't remain that way for much longer.

From the moment Egbert arrived there was trouble. He went very red when Mom hugged and kissed him at the airport and I could understand that. My mother overdoes hugging and kissing and she never cares who sees. But then Egbert took it out on me. As he shook my hand he slid his foot on top of mine and then stood hard on it.

"I'm pleased to meet you Samantha," he said in a loud voice so Mom and Dad would be impressed. "If you tell, I'll just say it was an accident," he whispered. I could feel the tears coming but had to hold them back as best I could while he grinned into my face. The pain was terrible. I was wearing flip-flops because it was Summer and as we walked out of the airport I tried to sneak a look at my injured foot. It was all red where he'd stood on it and there was definitely some blood near the nail on my big toe.

He never stopped calling me "Samantha" even though I asked him to call me "Sam" more than a hundred times. When we got home I had to show him around the house while Mom and Dad fixed a special welcome dinner.

I hated bringing him into my bedroom but it was the only way I could introduce him to Einstein.

Einstein's my pet mouse and if you close your eyes I'll describe him to you. My Dad told me Einstein was a very brainy scientist so my mouse is named Einstein because he's **very** intelligent.

He's the only one in our house who really listens to everything I say. He's so small that you can only stroke him with one finger. He's covered in tiny white hairs and always feels soft and warm. He has bright eyes like little beads and his nose and tail and the insides of his ears are pink. His tail is skinny like a pig's, but not squiggly. He lives beside my bed in a white cardboard shoe-box. He always squeaks "Hello" as soon as I walk into my bedroom but the day Egbert walked in with me, Einstein stayed silent. I should've known then, animals are very good judges of human beings.

And guess what Egbert did next? He picked Einstein up by the tail and started to **swing** him. Einstein squeaked the loudest I ever heard him. Then Egbert threw him back in his box.

"Ugly, isn't he?" he jeered.

I rushed to Einstein who was shivering in a corner. But he seemed to be alright.

"Don't you dare do that again! You could have broken one of his legs, you could have killed him! I glared ferociously at him but he only laughed.

"So what! Hey, can I play with that model airplane in the glass case?" He never even said "please."

"No, you can't. It was my Dad's when he was little and he says I'm not allowed to play with it till I'm thirteen and that won't be for another two months."

"Well, I'm thirteen. I can play with it."

"No, you can't. You might break it. It was Dad's special toy when he was little.

"If you don't let me play with it, I'll do something horrible to you."

I shivered when I saw how mean his eyes looked. Luckily Mom called us for dinner right then, but he pushed past me so hard on his way out that he nearly knocked me over.

He was a real goody two-shoes at the table, and he never slopped any of his food. Mom thought he was great.

"What a well-mannered boy you are, Egbert. Sam, you didn't wash your hands properly. Look at Egbert's. How clean they are!" The trouble with my mother is she only ever thinks about being CLEAN and saying PLEASE and THANK-YOU, like that should be the most important thing in a kid's life. She won't even come into my room any more unless I'm there, because she's afraid of Einstein.

After dinner my friend Jodie called for me. Of course Egbert had to come out to play with us as well. That was when two of the three really bad things happened. Jodie showed us

a beautiful stone she had found on the beach.
It had lovely sparkly bits that glistened when
you moved it. She left it on the window sill of
our house while we all went to climb the
garden wall. Later, when she was going home,
she went to collect it. It was GONE. Then
Egbert said in a real hard voice, "I SAW
SAMANTHA PUT IT IN HER POCKET."

I got such a fright I nearly choked trying to
get the words out.

"I did not! I never did! Honest, Jodie!" Jodie
stayed silent. I expected her to say she
believed me, but she didn't say anything. She
just stood, scuffing the grass with her foot,
her eyes all screwed up. I didn't like the way
she was looking at me so I held my arms out
wide. "Come on, you can search me to prove
it."

But before Jodie could move, Egbert dipped
his hand in the pocket of my shorts and when
he took it out, there was the little stone
sparkling in the palm of his hand.

"See, I told you! Samantha stole it!" he
shoved the stone into Jodie's hand.

"I didn't! I didn't! You must have put it
there to pay me back for not letting you play
with the airplane!" I turned to Jodie.

"Please, you've got to believe me! I'd never steal your stone."

But the horrible way Jodie was looking at me made me want to die. "You're a liar and a robber! I'll never play with you again. From now on I'll be best friends with Maura Campbell. I hate you!"

"Jodie, please come back! I didn't do it! I'll swear on the HOLY BIBLE..."

But she had run off before I could even finish speaking. I turned to Egbert. "This is all your fault! I'm going to tell on you."

He gave a nasty laugh, wriggling like a snake. "But you can't prove anything," he said and slunk off into the house. I dropped onto the grass and began to cry with my head down so nobody would see. I knew he was right. There was no point in telling. If your best friend won't believe you then what hope do you have with your mother? I couldn't blame Jodie for thinking I'd robbed her stone, not the way Egbert had made it all happen. Still, it hurt a lot that she wouldn't believe me.

Later I sneaked back into the house and up the stairs, not wanting anybody to see my red eyes. I knew if I told everything to Einstein, he'd help me feel better. But when I got to my room, EINSTEIN WAS GONE. His box was empty. I searched everywhere, even behind the skirting board where he'd once squeezed before, but I couldn't find him. My whole body was shaking, the way it does when you get a bad fright. I had this terrible feeling inside, all lonely and weird. It made me think that maybe I'd never see Einstein again, that he was gone forever.

"EINSTEIN! EINSTEIN! WHERE ARE YOU!" My shrieks and roars brought Mom and Dad running from the living room.

"Sam, what's the matter? Are you hurt? Stop screaming! You've woken Joey! Whatever is the matter?"

"Einstein! It's Einstein! He's MISSING!" I gasped for breath. "Missing?" My mother's face went white, like the way in a Tom and Jerry cartoon Jerry's face goes white when Tom sneaks up behind him and does something mean. Except my mother was no mouse. The truth is, she usually turned pale every time I tried to talk about Einstein. Only for my Dad, she'd never have let me get a mouse for a pet. Do you know what a phobia is? It's when you're afraid of something. Well, my Dad says my Mom suffers from MOUSEOPHOBIA. Anyway, this time she was paler than I'd ever seen her before.

"Missing? You, you mean he might be wandering around the house? That he's ... on the loose?" She looked like she'd seen a ghost.

"Oh, I knew I never should have let you get that mouse!" She turned to Dad. "George, he'll have to be found! I won't be able to sleep if he isn't. Good grief, he could end up in our bed!"

"If he does, Mom, the easiest way to catch him is to have a bit of cheese handy ..."

"Agh, stop it Sam, don't tell me any more!" Mom covered her ears with her hands. "George, he'll have to be found. NOW!"

"Okay, okay, take it easy Molly. We'll find him, don't worry." Dad turned to me. "Now, Sam, you and Egbert and Joey search upstairs. Your mother and I will look downstairs."

That was the great thing about my Dad. He could be pretty clever sometimes. Especially now, when there was an EMERGENCY.

All this time Egbert had stood leaning against the door of the spare room, saying nothing. I was surprised when he helped me to search, but not for long. Three times he kidded me that he'd found Egbert, but the third time was the worst.

"Hey, Samantha!" He came rushing into Joey's room where we were searching under the bed. "I've found Einstein! He's drowned in the bath! He must've fallen into Joey's bath water!"

I ran into the bathroom. But there was nothing in the bath except Joey's plastic duck. It took ten minutes before my heart stopped hammering. I hated Egbert. And to think I was going to have to put up with him for six whole weeks. It was then I made one of the most horrible wishes of my life. Here is what I wished. "ROLL ON THE END OF THE SUMMER HOLIDAYS." Can you imagine a kid wishing for such an awful thing?

But we never found Einstein. It was almost midnight when Dad called off the search. He had given Mom some wine, for medicinal reasons he said. She was smiling a lot when she came to say goodnight. I don't think she even NOTICED how red my eyes were. That night was the worst night of my life and the next three days were awful too. I searched and searched for Einstein but he was nowhere to be found. The only good thing that happened was that Jodie and I made up. Egbert had been jeering her out on the street and she'd soon got to see what he was like. The bad things that happened were that he kept on kidding me he'd seen Einstein. First he said Einstein was run over by a truck, then a road-roller, then eaten by the cat next door. After a while I stopped listening to him. I mean, I'm not THAT dumb.

Then, on the fourth morning after Egbert arrived we were all sitting having breakfast together when Egbert leaned over and whispered, "Hey, Samantha, Einstein's in the toaster. Your Dad's going to roast him when he makes his toast."

As I said, I'm not that dumb, but still I kept one eye on Dad as he put the bread in and switched on the toaster. Two minutes later there was a burning smell in the kitchen.

"That blooming toaster's jammed again," said my Dad, unplugging it and peering inside. "What the blazes …!"

I had to put my glass down because my hand was shaking so much the milk was slopping all over the place.

Dad turned the toaster upside down and shook it. Lots of crumbs showered out and then it happened. Out fell a PINK TAIL. It was all burned at one end.

That's when I started to scream, even though I wasn't allowed to.

"It's Einstein's tail! It's Einstein's TAIL. Oh poor Einstein!. He must be dead by now!"

"No, Sam, it's okay, really! There's no mouse in here. Honest. Look."

I stopped screaming and wiped my eyes. Dad and I looked into the toaster. It was empty. I started to breathe properly again. "But how the dickens did this get in there?" Dad picked up the burned tail and examined it. Then he sniffed it.

"Why, it's rubber," he said. "It just looks like Einstein's tail. But where did it come from?"

That was when I decided that tell-tale or not, I'd had enough of Egbert and his sick jokes.

"He did it!" I shrieked, pointing at Egbert. "It's all his fault!"

We all looked at Egbert, even Joey. Egbert's face turned bright red and then he said, "It was only a joke. I bought a rubber mouse in the joke shop yesterday. I just wanted to play a trick on Samantha."

My dad gave him his, "YOU'RE IN VERY SERIOUS TROUBLE" look, and said, "Come with me Egbert."

Everybody, even Joey, stayed very quiet while they left the kitchen. Then I told my mother everything that had happened since Egbert had arrived. I knew she was angry because her lips went very thin and straight. She said I should have told her what had been going on but I said nothing. She didn't even like it when I tried to talk to her about Einstein, so how could I have told her anything? And I couldn't tell my Dad because he had worked very late the last two nights. I had been asleep when he got home.

Dad and Egbert came back as we were clearing the dishes from the table. Egbert had his head down. It made him look different. Then I noticed he had something in his hand. It wriggled. "Egbert has something he wants to return to you, Sam."

I stared and stared. "Einstein? It's EINSTEIN." This time my scream was a happy one. It was the best moment in my life. "Where did you find him?" I lifted Einstein and rubbed him against my cheek. He squeaked. He knew it was me straight away. That's how clever he is.

"Egbert didn't find him, Sam. I'm afraid Egbert had Einstein in his room all along. He now has something to say to you."

I stared at Egbert. "You took Einstein? You KIDNAPPED him?

"Yes." Egbert kept looking down at his shoes.

Then I remembered something. "Was it because I wouldn't let you play with Dad's model airplane?"

"Yes. I'm sorry for everything I did." But he kept his head down and I couldn't see his face, so I didn't know whether he was really sorry or just saying it because Dad was standing beside him.

Still, after that things really improved. I even stopped wishing that the holidays were over. Egbert got friendly with a boy down the road and they mostly played together. So I didn't have to bother with him much. But from then on I kept my bedroom door locked, just in case. Well, wouldn't you?

Learning by Accident

Carolyn Swift

Learning by Accident
Carolyn Swift

"Will you get those books off the table this minute! Your father will be in for his tea."

Paula sighed. She was trying to write an essay on "Threats to Our Environment" and finding it difficult enough without yet another interruption.

"And you needn't be pulling faces either," her mother added. "I want that table laid. I've enough to do without having to see to every little thing myself. Has Jimmy his eckers finished?"

"Why don't you ask him?"

"Don't give me cheek! You needn't think you're too old for me to give you a good clatter that would put manners on you! Jimmy!"

Jimmy dragged his mind away from the telly for just long enough to reply.

"What is it, Ma?"

"Will you turn that telly down a bit. We can't hear our ears and you know your father always complains if it's too loud!"

Jimmy squeezed the remote control for a second, lowering the volume so little the difference was hardly noticeable, but his mother seemed satisfied. Paula knew he had not even started his eckers, but he never seemed to get screamed at. He was nearly nine now, but to his mother he was still the baby, to be petted. He had only to peep up at her through his thick black lashes to get the soft side of her.

Now he sniffed happily at the smell coming from the cooker and, without taking his eyes from Kylie Minogue and Jason Donovan, showed his appreciation.

"Mmm!" he said. "I love bangers and mash!"

As Paula stacked her books, she saw her mother beam at Jimmy as if he had just presented her with a big box of chocolates. Jimmy always seemed to do the right thing. It just wasn't fair.

If only her father were home more often. He always stood up for her. She wished he could be like all the other fathers in their street. They would be home every evening after work. Maybe sometimes they got screamed at for coming back late from the pub, especially on pay day, but at least they were not always going to meetings. It would be different, she thought, if her father worked nights the way Maggie's father used to do when he was with Johnston Mooneys, but then he had always been home when Maggie got back from school.

Her own father seemed to be out both day and night, Paula thought, as she took the knives and forks from the drawer. All day he would be out painting shops or people's houses but then, instead of being home evenings and weekends, a great deal of the time there would be meetings.

"It can't be much of a union," her mother would snap, "if they can't manage even one meeting without you!"

Her father would get angry then, and when he got angry his face grew red.

"Can you not get it through your head that I'm the shop steward?" he would shout. "Plus

I'm up for election for the committee of No. 9 Branch."

And, although Paula was disappointed that he was going out again, she would still feel annoyed with her mother too, because she ought to be proud of him for being so important in the union.

Paula had heard him speak at a street meeting once. It was to do with unemployment and she had swelled with pride at the way the men had all cheered him. He had made them laugh too. When one of the other men had been speaking, someone had kept heckling. When it came to her father's turn, he had soon put a stop to that. At the very first interruption he had turned to face the heckler and called him by name.

"You were probably still crying for your soother at the time, Joe," he had said.

A great shout of laughter had gone up from the crowd and the heckler had kept quiet after that. Paula had noticed how the men crowding around him had never taken their eyes from her father's face while he was speaking. He seemed to be able to make them react exactly the way he wanted.

Maybe other fathers were home every evening, but they could never do that! Her mother ought to realize that her father was special.

She was putting the cups into the saucers when she heard the sound of running feet outside in the street and her friend Maggie burst into the kitchen.

"Paula!" she shouted. "Will you come with me to see the Hothouse Flowers in the RDS?"

Paula looked at her as if she had taken leave of her senses.

"Are you bonkers?" she asked. "The tickets are thirteen pounds each!"

"I know," Maggie laughed, "but I just won two free ones in a competition."

"You didn't?"

"I did. I had to answer four questions about the Hothouse Flowers and my correct answer must have been first out of the hat!"

"Oh, Maggie, you're brill!" Paula screamed, and the two girls hugged each other and jumped up and down in excitement.

"Maybe Maggie's mother doesn't mind her going to that class of thing, but I'll not have you at it!"

Paula had forgotten everything else at the

thought of seeing her idols in person. Now her mother's words were like a shower of cold water.

"Ah, Mammy, please!" she pleaded.

"I said 'No!'"

"But why, Mammy?"

"There'll be crowds at it, and a rough bunch at that. I know the sort that goes to them old concerts—half-jarred before they get there and bringing in bottles by the neck, or worse!"

"Ah no, Mrs Flynn," Maggie intervened. "You're not allowed bring drink into the RDS."

But Paula's mother shook her head obstinately.

"You can save your breath to cool your porridge. I've seen too many getting carried out by the John's Ambulance."

"Ah, Mammy! That's only on the telly!"

"You're not going and that's that! I'm not having the guards knocking on *my* door to say my daughter's after being taken to the Meath!"

"Ah, Mammy!" Paula gave a wail of despair.

"Now what's wrong? Can I never come

home to my tea without there's someone giving out about something!"

It was her father's voice and Paula felt a sudden hope. She rushed over to him and caught his arm.

"Please, Dadda, can I go to see the Hothouse Flowers? Maggie's got two tickets and I want to go more than anything in the whole world?"

"What's it gonna cost me?"

"Nothing, Dadda. Honestly! The tickets are a terrible price but Maggie got them for free! Please, Dadda, say I can go!"

"I don't see why not, if the tickets are free!"

"Have sense, Christy!" her mother cut in. "You know the crowd you get at them old rock concerts. On drugs, the half of them. It's not safe for two young ones on their own."

"If you were talking about a pair of well-heeled, stuck-up teenagers from Foxrock, now, I'd agree with you," her father said, "but these young ones know what's what. They've surely sense enough to steer clear of trouble for one evening."

"Oh thanks, Dadda!" Paula flung her arms around his neck. "I promise not to get mixed up with any of the fellas that look like starting shenanigans!"

"It's not you that's going to be sitting up waiting and worrying," her mother snapped angrily at her father, but he only said: "Is the tea wetted? I've to go to a meeting."

Paula was so excited, thinking of the Hothouse Flowers, she hardly noticed the bitter things her mother said during tea about people who could never be satisfied with their own homes. Besides, she had heard them all before. She was not surprised when her father got to his feet without waiting for his usual second cup.

"You've a tongue sharp enough to drive any man from the door, Mary," he said, putting on his coat. "But I'm warning you: keep it off Paula!"

Then he went out, slamming the kitchen door after him.

Her mother wrenched it open again and ran out after him, her voice rising in anger.

"You needn't try to excuse your own wrong-doing by bringing Paula into it," she shouted. "I'll bring her up right in spite of you and your bad example!"

"And I'm telling you you'll be sorry yet if you don't leave her be!" her father shouted back. "She wouldn't be the first teenager to leave home over a nagging mother. There's girls not much older than her on the streets of London that took the boat for no better reason than the need for a bit of independence!"

When her mother came back into the kitchen, Paula was at the sink, rattling the cups in the basin and letting on not to have heard. It was easier that way.

She wished her mother and father were not always fighting. She was sometimes afraid when her father slammed out of the house that he might not come back. Then she would have no-one to stand up for her. If that happened, she thought, she might well leave home if she got half a chance. In the meantime, whenever her mother's voice started to rise, she just closed her eyes and thought of Liam Ó Maonlai, throwing back his head so that his hair swept his face. She would say and do nothing that might give her mother an excuse to stop her seeing the Hothouse Flowers.

There was less than a week to wait, but sometimes Paula felt as if Saturday would never come. When it did, she put on her favourite T-shirt, brushed her hair till it shone and ran around to Maggie's house the minute the tea was over.

" 'Bye, ma!" she had called out. "I'm off now."

"At this hour?" her mother had exclaimed, but she had not tried to stop her. Paula spent a lot of time around at Maggie's house and it had seemed safer to wait there, where nothing could go wrong with their plans.

There were crowds milling around the RDS when Paula and Maggie got off the bus in Ballsbridge and made their way over to the Simmonscourt Pavilion.

"Good thing we came early," Maggie said, looking up at the clouds darkening the sky over the showgrounds. "The rain's starting again. We'll only just get inside before it comes down."

They were held up at the entrance gates while everyone was searched to make sure they were not bringing drink in with them or anything that might get used as a weapon but, in the end, they found themselves in seats raised up high over on the right, but not too far back from the stage.

"They're good seats!" Paula said

delightedly. She would be able to see every expression on Liam's face from there.

"Hi, Maggie!" said a voice from behind them and, when Paula turned round to find out who it belonged to she saw Mick Burke. He lived around the corner from them, but he was also a lot older and had already started work for Mr. Meehan that owned the paint and wallpaper shop. She was surprised he would even bother talking to them, but then she remembered that Maggie was friendly with his sister Breda.

"Did you come into a fortune or what?" he asked, as Maggie returned his greeting, for he knew the girls were still at school, with no wages, like him, to buy tickets for rock concerts.

Maggie told him the whole story then: how she had gone on a message for her mother to her cousins, the Longs, who owned the paper shop and, while she waited for Gracie Long to pack up the messages, had been thumbing through a copy of 'U Weekly'. There had been a competition in it for two tickets and, without telling Gracie, she had torn out the page and entered.

"Some people have all the luck!" Mick said.

"The tickets cost an arm and a leg! I had to touch the old fella or I wouldn't even have had the price of a drink for tonight!"

"Shove up there, Mick," said a boy who was pushing his way into the empty seat behind them. He was tall with fair hair that reached almost to his shoulders and Paul thought he looked a bit like Liam.

"Well," he said, with a wink at Paula, "are you not going to introduce me to your friends?"

"They're just friends of my sister's," Mick told him. "That's Maggie and the one on the left's Paula."

"Hi, Maggie and Paula. Have a mint?" and the new arrival held out a packet so Paula could take one. "My name's Jim, by the way."

Suddenly Paula remembered where she had seen him before. He had been unloading rolls of wallpaper outside Mr. Meehan's shop a week ago and she had been so busy staring at him that she had tripped over a can of paint at the curbside. She blushed at the memory of it and mumbled her thanks as she popped a mint into her mouth. Then the big spots came up and she turned quickly to Maggie.

"They're going to start!" she said.

"Yeah, but there's another group on before the Flowers," Maggie warned, as the rest of the lights began to dim.

The support group was OK, but Paula was not bothered. The sound in the RDS was none too hot, she thought. Anyway, it was the Flowers she had come to see. She was conscious of Jim, sitting just behind her and was not sorry when the group finished their last number and the lights came up again. Ice-cream sellers took up positions in the aisles and little queues quickly formed in front of them.

A lot of people got up and left their seats, but Paula and Maggie sat on. There was not much point in moving around when they had no money to buy anything. She heard Jim and Mick leaving their seats. They were probably going to the gents. Boys always seemed to have to go more often. She watched them going down the steps towards the exit.

"He's nice, isn't he?" she whispered to Maggie.

"He's OK," she replied without much enthusiasm. "He's nicer when Breda's not there."

"Not Mick!" Paula retorted. "I mean Jim."

"I don't know anything about him," Maggie said. "He sounds a bit of a chancer!"

Paula's cheeks felt hot again. Jim had that same dreamy look that Liam had, as if he could see something far away in the distance. A chancer would never look like that!

"He was only being friendly," she said.

Then she broke off abruptly. They were coming back up the steps and Jim was carrying two tubs of ice-cream.

"Here, girls!" he said, holding them out. "Thought you might like a cooler!"

"Mmm, thanks!" Paula gasped. "I was dying for one!"

Maggie hesitated but Mick said: "Go on, Maggie. You might as well, seeing that he's already wasted his money!"

They had just scraped the last of the ice-cream from the tubs when the big spots came up again and this time there was a stir and a murmur of excitement ran through the crowd. Then the Flowers came on and Paula heard herself screaming with everyone else. The time went by quickly then, as they played number after number, while Liam threw his head back so that his hair fell across his face in the way Paula had so often pictured to herself. There was a lot of screaming and stamping and wolf whistles, but no fighting, and Paula thought how silly her mother had been to imagine that you could never have a rock concert without violence, just because of things she had seen on the telly from concerts in England or Slane Castle.

When it was clear that the Flowers were not coming back again, no matter how much they shouted, Paula and Maggie got up to go. Everyone was pushing and shoving then, in a hurry to get to the pubs or the head of the bus queue.

"Over here, girls!" Jim cried, pulling them in against the wall so that he and Mick were between them and a gang of boys who were climbing over the seats and thundering down the steps.

He steered them safely through the crowds that were pouring out through the exit doors into the drab outside world, where rain had turned the car park into a glistening lake.

"Now," he said, turning up his collar against the downpour, "who's coming for a jar?"

"Well, we aren't anyway!" Maggie told him

"They're under age and they've no money," Mick pointed out, as they began running towards the gates.

"There's no-one going to be looking at them under a microscope tonight," Jim grinned, "and I just robbed a bank!"

"Sooner or later Mr. Meehan's going to notice if pots of paint keep going missing," Mick warned, but Jim only laughed.

"If you're worried you can buy your own," he said. "Come on, girls!"

"We can't!" Maggie argued. "We've to get our bus."

"You'll be a long time waiting so," Jim said, as they turned the corner of the Simmonscourt Road. "Look at the queues!"

Paula saw then that they wound like snakes all the way along the railings of the show grounds. They would be drowned, she thought, and wished Maggie were not in such a hurry to get away.

"On the other hand," Jim continued, "if you stick around I'll drop you home. I've the van across in the car park of the Horse Show House."

"You'd be as well off inside as standing at the tail end of that length of a queue," Mick agreed. "The rain's getting worse."

It was true. The drops had been falling steadily, but now the wind was whipping it into their faces as they struggled against it in the direction of the bridge.

"There's no sense in standing out in this, Maggie," Paula pleaded. "Can't we go inside just while we'd be waiting?"

"If we can get in," Maggie said, for there were crowds milling around the door there too.

"We'll get in," Jim said. "I never yet knew a publican's till refuse silver!"

And in they squeezed, passed the dripping umbrellas and steaming jackets, into a corner near the door to the car park. It was good to be in out of the rain and amongst the crowd, all laughing and shouting. Paula thought again how silly her mother had been. True, the pub was uncomfortably full, with everyone pushing and shoving to try to get served, but they were all in good humour.

"What's it going to be?" Jim asked, as soon as they had found themselves standing room

"Can I have a vodka and white lemonade?"

Paula asked, trying to sound cool. She knew that was what the older girls at school usually asked for, and hoped Maggie would have the same, but she said she only wanted a coke. Jim protested that it was hardly worth the struggle to fetch her a coke, but she refused to change her mind.

"You might have kept me company!" Paula whispered, as the boys began fighting their way over to the bar.

"I like coke," Maggie said.

"So do I," Paula agreed, "but we don't want them thinking we're only kids!"

"I don't care what they think," Maggie said. "I wouldn't be here at all only for the rain. What would your mother say if she knew?"

"I don't care what she'd say!" Paula retorted. "If I listened to her I'd never have any fun. Da wouldn't mind me taking the odd drink."

She took a second and a third before she climbed, giggling, into the front of the van beside Jim, while the other two found room in the back amongst the rolls of wallpaper. The rain was still bucketing down as Jim waited his chance to pull out on to the

Merrion Road. They were in a queue of cars all trying to get out of the car park and there was a good deal of door slamming and confusion as people shouted their goodnights and tried to manoeuvre into position. There seemed to be an almost endless stream of traffic in the street and cars were only getting away one at a time. Finally, they reached the head of the queue.

"It's like looking into the fish tank down at the pet shop," Paula giggled, as she peered at the passing cars through the rain swirling down the windscreen. "I think we must be under the sea and those are all sharks and whales I can see in front of us!"

"You've crazy ideas in that little head of yours!" Jim laughed. "What else do you see?"

"Not much!" Paula said. "There are too many waves. I don't know how you can see where you're going!"

"That's only because the windscreen wiper on your side is banjaxed," Jim said. "I can see fine on this side."

There was a gap in the traffic then and he pulled out of the car park and became part of the swimming shoal. It suddenly struck Paula that it was ages since she had had tea and that she had been too excited to eat much even then.

"D'you know what?" she said. "I'm starving!"

"Right! We'll stop off at the chipper!" Jim swung the van over towards a fork in the road and a car honked angrily from behind. Jim laughed and honked back.

"What's he on about?" Paula giggled.

"He thought I was going straight on," Jim said, "but the chipper's this way."

Through the misty windscreen Paula saw a red light swimming ahead of them and felt the van slither sideways as it slowed.

"Bloody road!" Jim muttered. "It's a boat we need!"

But at that moment the light turned green and, instead of stopping, the van began gathering speed again. A pub door suddenly swung open and in the light it threw out, Paula suddenly saw shadows on the road in front of them. It was a second before she realized they were people, stepping off the curb carelessly, glasses in their hands.

Jim realized it at the same time and braked hard. The van skidded sideways and then there was a sickening crash as Paula was thrown forward with the force of the impact.

She was feeling sick. It was as if the crash had somehow happened inside in her stomach but, when she put her hand to it, not even her jeans were split. She could feel no pain at all, apart from the heaving inside.

Thanks be, she was not hurt. Then she looked down and saw her right knee. The denim was ripped apart and soaked in blood. Still, it could not be bad or she would feel pain. She must get home at once and wash the blood off before her mother could see it. She knew that and yet she still felt unable to move, just as she had sometimes done in nightmares.

She noticed then that there was broken glass everywhere. The windscreen must have smashed and that was why there was wet on her face. Then she heard the ambulance. She hated the sound and it seemed to be getting louder and louder. It stopped quite suddenly, as if the siren had snapped off. She heard voices. The man was only trying to help her, she realized that, but he might tell her mother. It would be better not tell anyone her name. She would just slip away on her own.

She caught the word "hospital" and found her voice. It sounded a little odd but it was definitely hers.

"I don't want to go to hospital," the voice said. "I'm all right. I'll just go on home."

The man was kind but he seemed to take no notice. Paula felt herself being lifted from the van and, just as in her nightmares, she seemed unable to struggle.

"You'll be with your friends," the man said, and only then did Paula see Maggie being helped into the ambulance in front of her. How selfish of her to have forgotten about Maggie.

"Is she hurt?" she cried anxiously.

"She's going to hospital just to be on the safe side, same as you," the man said reassuringly, and he set her down on a seat beside Maggie.

She felt better then, because she knew that if Maggie had been bad she would have been put lying down, like the man had been. Then it dawned on her the man was Jim. She hoped he was all right, though none of this would have happened only for him.

All of a sudden, she felt an ache in her

right knee. She supposed the cut would be deepish, to have bled so much. Still, if she ran cold water on it and put on some plaster, it would be fine and never show under her jeans. Then she remembered they were torn and bloodstained. Maybe it was just as well they were going to the hospital rather than straight home. She would get a chance to rinse them out and dry them before her mother saw her. Someone there would surely lend her a needle and thread.

"Are you OK?" Maggie whispered.

"I'm fine," Paula whispered back. "Only Mammy's going to kill me if she finds out. How about you?"

"I'm OK, only for my arm. I think I must have put it up to save my face."

How, Paula wondered, had she not noticed before that Maggie's arm was bent up in a funny way.

"Am I stupid or what?" she asked herself, but out loud she said nothing. Talking suddenly seemed a terrible effort. Maggie said nothing more either and they both sat staring in front of them until the ambulance stopped. When the doors opened, Maggie saw in the distance the gates of the Meath

Hospital.

"Oh no!" she cried, remembering what her mother had said when she had wanted to stop her going to the concert, "Not the Meath!"

Then she was lifted out of the ambulance, sat into a wheelchair and pushed up a ramp into a long, low building, rather like a hut. It was certainly not the main building, with its great stone steps leading up to a big imposing door that Paula remembered from the time they had come to visit her granny before she died.

As she was wheeled in, a nurse hurried over, holding a printed form, and asked her for her name and address.

"Do I have to say?" Paula asked, her teeth chattering. She suddenly felt very cold. The nurse looked at her impatiently.

"We have to get your parent's consent to your treatment," she said. "Don't give me a hard time. We're rushed off our feet tonight."

Paula's knee was hurting much more now. It seemed too much of an effort to argue. It would be her father who would come in any case. Her mother would not want to leave Jimmy alone in the house at night. She was still answering the nurse's questions as she was wheeled into Casualty.

She was put lying down on a hard, high bed which was on wheels and there was a man in a white coat. A light was switched on, so bright it reminded Paula of the big spots in the RDS. The man in the white coat bent over her and she suddenly felt a tearing pain in her knee and cried out.

"Be a good girl now!" the man said. "We have to get out all the bits of broken glass."

Paula bit her lip and dug her finger-nails into the palms of her hands. She was glad she could not see him probing the wound, searching for each tiny fragment of shattered windscreen. She felt glad, too, that she had given her address to the nurse. She wanted her father to come now, to feel his arms around her, comforting her, making her feel safe.

"That's clean now. It only needs stitching," the doctor said, and Paula's relief that the probing was over was short-lived. Although she tried hard to be brave, she cried out several times as the wound was sewn up. Would her father never come? It was not far to the Meath from their little house near the

Four Courts: only just across the Liffey, under the arch of Christ Church Cathedral. along Nicholas Street and through St. Patrick's Close. You could walk it in twenty minutes. She was sobbing now.

"All over!" the doctor said finally, just as she felt she could bear it no longer. Then she heard her mother's voice. It echoed shrilly from outside, just as it had so often done when Paula had overheard her giving out to her father.

"Where is she?" she was demanding loudly.

Paula's heart sank still further. She had wanted her father there to comfort her. Instead, her mother had come to give out to her. But when she was wheeled out of Casualty, her mother did not scold her at all. She kept hugging Paula and she was crying.

"Thanks be to God you weren't killed!" she kept saying. "Thanks be to God!"

Maggie's father was there too and, while the nurse gave her mother some tablets for her to take when she got to bed, Maggie came out of another door with her arm in a sling. Paula wanted to ask why her father had not come, but she was afraid to ask in front of Maggie's father. He had got them a taxi and Paula expected her mother to give out about the cost, but she never said a word.

She expected her father would be waiting for them but, when they got home, it was Maggie's father that carried her into the house.

"Where's Da?" she asked her mother, the minute he left.

"Where d'you think?" her mother replied wearily, going to fill the kettle and set it to boil. "He had 'a meeting'!"

"But it must be near morning!" Paula said in surprise.

There was bitterness in her mother's voice when she answered, but she spoke quietly.

"*Sunday* morning!" she said. "It's not the first time and I doubt it'll be the last."

At that moment, Paula heard her father at the door. She was going to call to him when she heard him trip over an empty milk bottle and curse. His voice sounded thick and strange.

While she hesitated, he lurched into the room, blinking at her foolishly. Even at that distance, Paula could smell the mixture of whiskey and cheap perfume. His shirt was crumpled, his hair tousled and there was a smudge of lipstick on his collar.

"What's wrong?" he muttered. "What's wrong?"

Was this her wonderful father that all the men looked up to? He was no different from the drunks that fell out of the pubs at closing time. But it was not closing time now and he looked more like someone who had fallen out of bed.

Suddenly Paula remembered what her mother had said to him about people who were never satisfied with their own homes. She thought of all the times she had needed him when he had not been there. And tonight, when she had needed him most of all, he had not been there either. She had wanted him to hold her, to comfort her, to tell her everything was all right.

Supposing, she thought, her mother sometimes felt like that too. She remembered, suddenly, a time when Jimmy was little more than a baby. He had screamed all evening and then there had been a power cut. There were wet clothes everywhere and her mother had no way of getting them dried. Her father had not told her then that everything was all right. He had got straight up and gone out, saying that he had a meeting. Her mother never had meetings though. She had to be there all the time. It could not be much fun for her, Paula thought.

It was at that moment that her father noticed the plaster on her knee.

"What did you do to yourself?" he muttered, stumbling across the room and clutching at the knee.

Paula yelled with pain.

"Don't touch me!" she screamed.

Her father fell back in surprise.

"All right! All right!" he mumbled. "No need to take the nose off me!"

Her mother came over then and Paula was afraid she would start shouting at her father. Instead, she took him by the shoulders and pushed him towards the door.

"Go to bed, will you?" she said wearily. "We've had troubles enough for one day!"

She spoke as if her father were a bold child, Paula thought. She expected him to get angry with her mother, but to her surprise he looked relieved.

He was like a child that realized he might not be punished after all. As her mother came back into the room, Paula could hear her father falling up the stairs.

"I'm sorry, Mammy!" Paula said. "It wouldn't have happened only for the rain."

Her mother simply poured a cup of tea and handed it to her.

"Ah well," she said, "you'll know better the next time, won't you?"

Paula nodded.

"I will, Mammy," she said. "I promise. I'll know better about a whole lot of things."

The Picnic

Anne Roper

The Picnic
Anne Roper

"I'm scared what'll happen unless we get someone to find Joe in time." Pauline's voice sounded funny, sort of squeezed and whispered. "If some crazy white man hears of it, Lord knows what he'll do."

Young Marsha could see Pauline and Tina through the screen door of the kitchen, her face pressed hard against its bellied middle. She was thinking that when the two coloured maids talked together, they spoke a strange and special language you couldn't always understand, though you knew the music. They were probably going on about one of their soap operas: 'Edge of Night' or 'Search for Tomorrow'.

"Can't see why you stick with that man sometime," she heard Tina reply. "All he ever do is bring you trouble." Marsha guessed something wasn't right from the rhythm of Tina's speech, but her own plans were far too important to delay listening further: Pat and Pam Scranks were going on a picnic to the Chickasaw Woods and Mrs. Scranks said Marsha could tag along. "If you git your own sandwiches. I ain't runnin no restaurant round here, servin lunch to the whole neighbourhood."

Saturday plans like these were generally spur of the moment. In this case, the Scranks twins had been driving their mother crazy most of the morning, in and out of the porch, slapping the back door, letting flies in, making lemonade and racket. Marsha had spied all the activity through the mesh of a cyclone fence that bounded her backyard.

"Where ya'll going?" she'd hollered as the Scranks, in single file, passed her gate. Mrs Scranks' off-hand reply had been all the invitation she needed.

"Tina, hey! Scranks are having a picnic and I can go if I bring my own lunch." The kitchen door banged shut as Marsha slid across the linoleum. She began tugging at the bread drawer, freeing a white loaf wrapped in waxed paper. Next, she scraped a step ladder over to the pantry and pulled down a jar of peanut butter. "Quick, Tina. Help or I'll be too late. Twins'll be nearly there by now."

Tina Crump had been minding the Poplar children since the eldest was in diapers and knew each one like her own. She switched off the iron and looked down.

"What you after? Can't you see we talking?" A sudden electrical shudder settled the refrigerator into a routine hum.

"But—"

"But nothin. Pauline and I have business to finish, honey. Grown-up business. You just run along outside for a few minutes and I'll make you a sandwich with some egg salad I did this morning." Tina crouched down on the floor now, eye-level with the child. To Marsha she looked like a zebra, the sun slicing through wooded shutters on to her dark skin.

"They say you shouldn't eat eggs in heat like this," Pauline's words pressed cold between them. "Not boiled ones, anyhow. Say they go bad—make you sick."

"Pooh." Marsha darted to the ice-box and opened it. "Big fat Tom Hooten ate a stink-bug once and they taste just like hard boiled eggs. That's why he smells like you-know-what!"

"Don't you go messin with that big boy now, he's as near to low down as I know in a child his size." Tina's regular warning about the eldest Hooten forced a whoop of laughter out of Marsha, so great she had to kneel down on one leg in case she'd wet her pants. She didn't care that the two women had stopped paying her any mind. She was used to it: "Think they'd run out of things to jabber on about," she overheard her mother once, "expect that man of Pauline's knocked sense from her long ago." So Marsha busied herself rummaging in the fridge until her hands came across the bottle she wanted.

"Here—Mommy said I could have some coke for lunch today." It was a fib, but Tina might believe her.

"Uh-uh, no ma'am. All I need is for you to come home cut up from splits of glass. Lemme put it in something safe." While Tina spoke, Pauline moved to the far side of the room. She paused for a few moments studying Marsha's younger brother as he fussed in the crib. "Go ahead and tend to that girl," Pauline's words came out in a burst, like she was snuffing a candle. She bent to lift the noisy, tiny form: "I'll tend to this one til you're ready."

* * * * *

Noon is the hottest time of the day in that neighbourhood. It's when tar in the street starts to bubble and dogs seek the shelter of persimmon trees or babies get put down to nap. When she was even smaller, Marsha climbed out the bathroom window and sat in some tar to see if she would stick. She'd seen Little Wheezer's big sister trap him like that in 'Our Gang' on the television, and was experimenting so the same thing would never happen to her. But when her father found out, she got ten whacks with a willow switch.

Another time she opened a dozen eggs on the sidewalk to see if they would fry in the heat. "You're trying me, child," Mr. Poplar sighed as his cross, big hands pinned her to an armchair until she apologized.

Once, when Pam Scranks was stung by a bumble-bee, Marsha carefully picked most of the petals from her father's pink roses to make a cushion for her friend's sore hand. This time her daddy pinched her by the wrist and popped her with a fly-swatter; unable to

free herself, Marsha hopped around him
yowling: a spoke to the hub of his wheel

"He didn't mean no harm," Tina explained
later. "Grown-ups have to teach kids about
protecting living things." She was showing
Marsha how to make a canasta cake and bent
to let her lick the spoon. "Thinks you'll learn
what's right from wrong that way, I guess."

That had been a hot day too, and after
supper, when everyone had gone to sleep, the
smell of the remaining roses reached Marsha
through the open bedroom window.

*   *   *   *   *

Today the heat was so persistent that once
Marsha headed off, Tina had to root out the
electric fan from its winter place in the car-
port. "With such a hot spell now, no tellin
what summer'll do." She was trying to
distract Pauline from her worry.

"If somethin don't happen soon, I'm going
up to find him—"

"You trying to scare me, girl? You staying
right her til we know what's what."

"No, I ain't." Pauline tried to pass Tina, felt
resistance, then gave up and returned to
pacing the kitchen floor. "You got any

tobacco?" She reached for Tina's pocket-book.

"Don't be a fool. No sense in starting a bad habit just 'because'."

Pauline turned to the table and switched on the radio. The broadcast came in scratchy at first—distant and difficult to understand. Tina had to stretch across to tune the local station.

"There's a knack to it," she explained as the news began; it seemed an incident up in Bellevue Lawns was being investigated by the police. A Mrs. Odell Butler had been admitted to Baptist Hospital in serious condition, while a negro, male, early thirties was wanted for questioning. As the sports results came on, a blue-bottle beat frantically against the lining of the sugar bowl; the weather forecast followed: humid, unsettled, with a chance of thunderstorms later.

* * * * *

Leaving the heat of the neighbourhood for the canopy of birch and poplars, Marsha felt a coolness, then quiet. She loved the woods. Tina said the grounds had once been part of the Chickasaw plantation, first owned by Indians and later by rich white folks. Now the big house was deserted and tumble-down, the lands gone wild.

With a good way to go before she reached the picnic site, Marsha was already feeling hungry. She chewed a bit at the crust of her sandwich, to keep her until she met up with the Scranks. While juggling the bread and brown paper bag, she began humming 'Purple People Eater'. When she fought with her older brother, she called herself the 'Purple People Beater,' until he threatened to beat her purple if she didn't lay off.

It was her brother who first showed her the woods. She was six and he'd scared her by dangling her over the 'crocodile pit'—an old root cellar covered by rotting boards. Later, when they approached the empty house, he'd bragged it was a murder mansion where negro slaves had been roasted alive, their eyes plucked out by giant tweezers.

Now grown-ups were rarely seen in the woods—except for the Baptists who put up a great tent each year and ran vacation bible school on summer mornings, revivals at night. Mrs. Poplar said it was a sin for Catholics to attend Protestant services like theirs, but Marsha had snuck into several classes. She'd enjoyed singing 'Jesus Loves Me' and colouring pictures of St. Francis of Assisi. Afterwards, she'd worn her brother's scapular, the one that protected you from hell for 500 years, so she wasn't really worried about damnation.

The only thing that really scared her these days was Crazy Roy, the ghost of a slave who haunted the outhouses attached to the big house. To avoid being captured and eaten alive, you had to run past them as fast as you could, holding your breath.

On her own, Marsha hesitated, unable to figure out how best to manage the lunch bag (it was tearing from the weight of the Thermos and the moisture in her hands). Finally she took a deep breath and bolted for the far side. Half-way beyond, her foot caught something hard, sending her stumbling across the gravel, shattering the Thermos on impact.

* * * * *

It was a few seconds before Marsha found all her breath. First she examined her scratched knee, licking away balls of blood that rose to the surface. Then she looked

around for her lunch things and rubbed aside
a few angry tears; the remains of her
sandwich now lay mushed in the dirt. "Who
wants to go on a stupid old picnic anyway,"
she reasoned. The Scranks would probably be
heading back soon, and if they found her here,
hanging around, they'd call her chicken for
not following. Marsha decided it was better to
hide in the kudzu beyond and keep a look-out.
Then she could jump on the twins as they
passed and scare *them* silly for a change.

Quickly she gathered up the broken flask
and hid it in the clump of shrubs near the
back of the house. She could say she lost it
and ask Tina to explain what happened to her
mother. "It's her fault I had it the first place."
Marsha scuffed her left shoe against some
stones.

Suddenly, her attention was drawn to a
movement inside the house, a shadow beyond
the frame of the lowest window. Her first
reaction, thinking it was the twins, was to call
out, but something made her pull back an
instant, to listen. First she thought she heard
wheezing, then a heavy noise, like dragging.

"I'm not afraid of no dumb ghost," she told
herself as she stood tip-toe and stretched her

neck for a closer look. One of the panes was missing, but she knew if she balanced herself carefully, she just might be able to see inside.

Inching her head through the opening, she jumped as a burst of thunder erupted overhead. Then came Crazy Roy's face, jutting at her through the gap, moaning like some monster jack-in-the-box, only sweating, torn, and gouged with red.

Marsha didn't look back once as she scrambled to escape. In the pandemonium that followed, the thought of his footsteps and the sound of her heart beating got all mixed up. She was certain he was right behind as she crashed through the underbrush. "Don't let him get me," she whispered, tearing past prickly weed and fallen branches. "Please don't let him get me!" And in all the confusion, cicadas scratched out their high-pitched alarm.

* * * * *

"How do you know they mean Joe? He ain't never had no business up in the Lawns," Tina's tone was sharper than she meant. She was trying to hide her growing anxiety.

"He got some yard-work choppin weeds last week and the lady up there been giving him the run-around about paying. So he's been up everyday, trying to git it outa her," Pauline's voice wavered. "Then he didn't come home last night. Thought he'd gone over cross the river to the dog track and got to drinking—but he'd be back by now ..."

"You sure it's the same woman? They's plenty up in Bellevue. He ever mention this Mrs. Butler?"

Pauline let go some air, bobbing her head between her hands.

"Well it ain't no use asking my Floyd to go up and check on him. If they looking for a black man, any one'll do—they ain't fussy."

Tina poured another glass of iced tea, spilling the last drops down the side, onto the table. Pushing the drink aside, she lit herself a cigarette. Pauline took out a handkerchief and wiped her eyes, then daubed at the necklace of perspiration circling her throat.

"Waiting, that's what kills you ... not knowin what's goin on and no way to stop it from happenin." On the far side of the room the Poplar baby wriggled restlessly after its bottle, tiny hot limbs sticking, then sucking free of the plastic sheet beneath.

* * * * *

Except for the occasional judder of thunder in the distance, everything was still where Marsha hid. She didn't know how long she'd been kneeling in the thicket; all she knew was she was feeling less afraid. From this spot, the old house was no longer visible. Behind her, where the creeping plants thinned out, a grove of evergreens and oaks sheltered a floor of soft pine needles. Marsha walked over and sat down. Then she lay on her back and looked up at the blackening sky. If it rained, she be protected here; besides, she liked storms.

Secure in her surroundings, she began planning what she'd do to whoever played Crazy Roy on her: "Think they can fool me with some old trick like that. I'm gonna get Mrs. Scranks to whupp those twins good— th'ain't no such things as ghosts." She repeated this last thought several times until the closeness of the day pressed her gradually into sleep.

It was an abrupt poke in the shoulder not long after, that wakened her. Tommy Hooten stood looking down, a long blade of grass trapped between uneven teeth: "Better be careful out here. Nigger's on the run and he's liable to sneak up on you like I did and slit your throat."

"Hey, Tom." Marsha moved back a little before standing. For a minute she'd forgotten why she was here, forgotten her recent fear at the window. "What you doing in the woods?"

"Huntin." He smiled broadly. "My daddy says this coon done attacked a lady up in the Lawns. Says this nigger ought to be strung up." The boy shoved a thick hand deep into his pocket and pulled out a boy-scout knife. "I'm gonna catch him and get me a re-ward."

At thirteen, Tommy was older than Marsha. More than once she'd seen him grab smaller kids in his front yard and tack them to the ground, saying he'd snip off their ears next time they trespassed. In braver times, she'd chanted "Rootin Tootin Tommy Hooten," as she ran past the house—especially when she was pretty sure no one was home. Marsha had never been alone with him.

"I'd better be gettin ... went on a picnic with Scranks, and Tina said I was to come home straight after ... "

"There's a bird nest over yonder," Tommy pushed his face into hers. "I know cause I climbed that tree th'other day and found it. Baby chicks there too, I'll show ya." His free hand closed over her wrist. Marsha noticed his fingernails were chipped and dirty.

But she was curious about the nest. Once with the Scranks, she'd found a jay's egg in the school playground and brought it home to see if it would hatch. She lined a corner of her underwear drawer with tin foil and cotton, but the smell after a few days made her mother flush it down the commode.

"Let me see too. I can't reach," Marsha complained as Tommy shimmied up the trunk of the oak. She noticed the back of his neck was already sunburnt and spotted with freckles.

"Hang on, I'll give you a boost." He hopped down to offer his cupped hands as step-up. For a second she hesitated, suspicious in case he'd drop her for the joke. But once up, his grip was steady.

Although Marsha was excited about seeing the newborns, she was careful not to get too close. Tina told her that you shouldn't fool with a bird's nest because the mother would smell you near and leave the chicks: "They call it tainting—like poison everywhere you touch."

As Marsha inched her way gingerly up the tree, she felt heat as bark rubbed against skinned knee. When she could almost see into the nest, she heard tiny cheeps, and by the time she'd come eye-level, the chicks were screeching.

Marsha had never seen anything like it.

One of the eggs was still whole, the baby birds nothing more than pink skin, with out-stretched necks and thumb-nail beaks. Marsha was busting to touch one, but Tommy Hooten grabbed at her leg and dropped her with a jolt.

"Give me another look. I'm the one who found them." His face was pudgy and hot, with smudges of grease on one cheek.

"You're not meant to pick em up, Tommy ... "

"You're can't tell me what to do." He cracked a stick and waved it over her. "I can pick 'em up and play with 'em or whatever I like, and nobody, specially not a baby like you, can make me do anything I don't want."

What happened next came to Marsha strangely, as if she was looking through a net, or watching a movie on the TV, and there was nothing she could do to make it stop: first the boy reached in among the twigs, removed something, and threw it past her with such great force, it hit another tree and smashed, spilling yellow and brown liquid in streams down the bark. Next he straddled a bough, picked out one chick and held it high for Marsha to see. Then with one swift slice, he severed the creature's head from its body and tossed the separate pieces at Marsha's feet.

"See! I can do whatever I want. And if you tell anyone, I'll do it to you." Somewhere in the distance, Marsha could hear crows screaming, then a cloudburst, and the sound of rain breaking through the branches.

*   *   *   *   *

The telephone rang several time before Tina could bring herself to answer. The kitchen, recently darkened in the sudden shower, now brightened as the afternoon sun erased shadows from the room. Pauline stood at the window staring out across the lawn, the hem of her dress batting gently against her legs in the new breeze.

"Yeah, I know ... I'll tell her. Ain't nothin else you coulda done," Tina glanced across at Pauline. Her friend was standing with her forehead pressed against a pane of glass. As Tina spoke, her hands clutched at the sill for support.

"County or City? Sure ... you be careful comin home now. Don't worry none about us. It'll be an hour at least before someone can make it down, with buses like they is. I got to stay here til Mrs Poplar gets home." She put down the receiver and turned to face Pauline. Her friend spoke first:

"Joe's dead, ain't he?"

"No he ain't—not yet anyway." Tina stepped to the table, lit another cigarette and handed one to Pauline. "Floyd says the police caught a gang trailing him up the far side of the woods. Some neighbour of that Butler woman saw him headed through the back and put two and two together, kicking up an almighty ruckus. But somebody must've got to him. Sheriff found him all busted up near Chickasaw House. Unconscious, Floyd says. They took him to City Hospital." She paused.

"Don't look like that girl. You ain't going down there on your own—"

But Pauline had stopped listening. She was searching through her purse. "Th'aint enough here for the transfer ... takes two buses to get downtown. You got twenty cents to lend me?"

Tina turned away.

"Whether you help me or not, I'm going." But before Tina could argue, the telephone cut in again, waking the baby. It was the Scranks twins calling: now that they were back from the picnic, could Marsha come over and play?

*   *   *   *   *

In the few minutes before the midtown bus arrived, Tina had time to diaper the infant, settle him on his stomach, and begin worrying about Marsha. During the time it took to walk to the edge of the lawn, she left the child, watching Pauline board the bus just before it pulled away; then she began calling for Marsha, finding her eventually under a clump of rose bushes near the water spiggot vomiting. The girl was shaking in the heat and her clothes felt damp.

"Never shoulda given you those eggs," Tina murmured to herself as she guided Marsha slowly inside to the bathroom. "Looks like Pauline was right all along." There she pulled over a small stool and sat the child down next to the toilet: "Use the bowl if you feel sick again, baby." She draped a towel around the girl's shoulders, gently stroking the back of her neck until the convulsions eased.

"That's better now. You alright?"

When at last she had calmed, Marsha looked up. In her sudden hurry to speak, she stuttered the first words, "S ... s ... s ... something happened in the woods today, Tina—"

The woman's large hands pulled the child close, "I know, sugar, I know."

Summers Are Best

Michael Scott

Summers are Best
Michael Scott

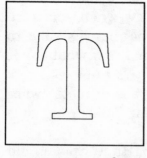

he old man he met the second time he ran away told him that summers were best.

During the summer you could sleep in the park, or in doorways or, if you were close to the sea, you could sleep on the beach, although even the softest sand grew hard after a few hours. The old man was full of stories, and he taught Spider a lot about surviving on the streets. And, although Spider knew the man on and off for nearly two months, he never did discover his name.

But the streets were like that. It was easy to drift into a casual friendship, and just as easy to drift out of it as well.

The first time Spider had run away he had managed to remain "free" for nearly three

189

days. The second time he had been out for nearly a month—although it actually felt longer. It was difficult to tell time without a watch. After the first few days you soon lost track of the time; you knew when you were hungry and you knew when it was time to sleep. Soon, you didn't even know what day it was ... except for Sunday. You always knew when it was Sunday: the streets were quieter, and the church bells rang out unceasingly.

This was now the third time Spider had run away from home. He wasn't even sure why he did it anymore, except that he liked the freedom and the excitement. He had been away from home for nearly three months now ... but it felt like years. He had run away in early June, shortly before the school exams— he knew he wouldn't do well anyway—and it was now late August. It had been a good summer; the weather had been very good, warm and dry with not too much rain, and there had been plenty of tourists, and some of them had been generous to the young boy begging on the bridge. Spider felt no shame in begging—it was the only way he had of making any money. The problem was that there were far too many others begging on Dublin's streets, and there just weren't enough tourists, and not enough money to go around. The boy also knew that people grew tired of beggars; once they had seen a few, and perhaps even given them money, they were not so generous with some of the other street people. But now, at the end of August the numbers of tourists were diminishing, and already there was a touch of Autumn in the air—he felt it in the mornings, and it was colder in the evenings, and he supposed it was time he started thinking about the oncoming winter. He found he didn't want to spend a winter on the streets. Maybe that unnamed old man had been right: summers were best.

Spider leaned back against the metal rail of the Ha'penny Bridge, his eyes half closed against the glare of the late evening sun. There was a cardboard box in his hand, with three single pennies lying in the bottom of it. There was close to two pounds in his pockets though, so it hadn't been a bad day. The trick was not to leave too much money in the box at any one time: if you left too much, people would be less inclined to give, or some of the other beggars would steal it from you, but if you left nothing in the box, people knew you were taking it all out anyway.

A young couple passed by quickly, neither of them looking at him, both deeply engrossed in conversation. Young people gave less; he didn't know whether it was because they had less to give, or because they didn't care, but nowadays he didn't even bother asking, "Spare some change, please?"

He closed his eyes, the evening sunlight warm and orange against his eyelids, feeling peaceful and contented. He had enough money for food and a bed for the night—what more could someone ask for?

Hearing solid footsteps on the bridge he opened his eyes and spotted the two tourists coming towards him. Spider was an expert on tourists—the types who gave, and those who ignored him. Elderly, female Americans were his favourite; sometimes—and he was unsure if it was because they were unfamiliar with the money—they gave out pound notes. He opened his eyes wide, tilted his head downwards and looked up with his best sorrowful expression on his face. He waited until he caught the woman's eye.

"Spare some change please," he whispered, his voice just loud enough to be heard but still managing to sound low and dispirited. Looking vaguely embarrassed the woman fumbled in the pocket of her long plastic raincoat and dropped two coins into his box. Still watching her intently, he whispered, "God bless you," and then waited until they had gone before looking into the box. A fifty and twenty pence piece; this was going to be one of his better days. Spider knew one of his great advantages was his appearance; he was small and slender, his bare arms bony and angular, his collarbones and ribs visible beneath the dirty teeshirt he wore. His pale hair was spiky—he knew it was fashionable now, but with him it was just because it hadn't been washed in nearly three months, and his eyes seemed far too big for his small face.

He passed his hand over the money and the two coins disappeared, leaving only the three pennies in the bottom of the box. Closing his eyes again, he settled back against the rail to wait. But he made no more money that night.

Spider finally left his post when the sun sank and a chill breeze began to whip up the river, reminding him once again that perhaps it was time to think about going home. As he crossed the bridge and turned to the left, heading down the quays towards Westmoreland Street and one of the fast-food restaurants there, he suddenly realized that he was a little luckier than most of the other runaways. At least he still had a home he could go to. A lot of the other boys—and girls too, and there seemed to be more and more girls recently—had no homes to go back to, or if they did have homes, the situations there made going back impossible.

The first time he had run away had been shortly after his mother had remarried. He supposed it was his step-father's fault, although the man had done nothing to him— nothing except take his mother away, he thought. Ever since his father died five years previously, he had grown very close to his mother, and he resented this other man coming into her life and doing all the things he used to do. And yet his step-father had been very kind to him, very understanding too when Spider had shouted and sworn in the house. He had paid the bills when Spider had got into trouble with the law and been caught breaking and entering a local shop. His mother though had been less understanding and it was following a huge row with her that he had first run away. He remembered thinking as he slipped out shortly after midnight that this would be a lesson to her; she hadn't cared for him, so at least this way she would have to think about him.

Spider stopped, looking in the Virgin shop window, not looking at the displays of record sleeves, seeing only his own reflection in the glass. Had he once thought that about his mother? He titled his head to one side considering, and then nodded fiercely at himself. He had.

Digging his hands deeply into his pockets, he turned to the right into Westmoreland Street, wondering where he was going to eat tonight. While all of the fast food restaurants served people like him—the street people—very few of them allowed them to eat in the restaurant itself: it was bad for business. Anyway, he didn't like eating in the restaurant, he preferred his own company. He'd get something and eat it in one of the quieter backstreets and then head back into the city centre to wait for the cinema and theatre crowd—they were usually good for a few shillings. Theatres were a better mark, he knew; all those people in their fancy clothes liked to be seen to be giving—or perhaps they just gave because they felt guilty. Either way he didn't care, so long as they gave.

Spider's stomach began to rumble the moment he stepped into the burger restaurant. This was his first and only meal of the day: breakfast and lunch were cans of coke and a bar of chocolate. He didn't really like burgers, but when you were hungry everything tasted good and he never had enough money to buy anything else.

As he waited in the line he remembered the first time he'd run away. He had been hungry most of the time then—he didn't know how to beg properly, didn't know which restaurants threw out food in the morning. Then, he'd spent a lot of time thinking about his mother's cooking. He thought about her cooking now. It was funny—you never really missed home until you were away for a time! He had become so used to being dirty and always a little tired and more than a little hungry that he sometimes forgot what it was like before, when he had a room of his own, a soft bed, food and hot, hot water.

He ordered quickly and noticed with a smile how his meal was placed in a bag to take away, while the young man on his left, who couldn't have been very much older than himself was asked, "Eat here or take away ...?" He had the exact amount of money ready, so there was no waiting around for change, and was already eating his chips before he reached the door. He chewed everything carefully before swallowing each mouthful, knowing if he bolted the food he would have hiccups for the rest of the night.

Spider wandered back into the city centre, the bag clutched close to his thin chest, feeling the heat seep through the paper and his dirty cotton teeshirt.

There wasn't really any reason for him to keep running away, but there wasn't any real reason for him to stay at home either. All he ever did was go from home to school and back to home again. He was too independent for friends, got bored too easily to do well in school; he needed the excitement of being on the streets, living by his wits. Every day was different, every day brought new challenges, new excitement thrills.

Spider finished the chips—which grew colder more quickly—and started on the burger. Mind you, this time hadn't been as much fun as the last time. Probably because he knew the ropes, knew his way around. He hadn't made any friends on the streets this time. The type of runaway on the streets had changed too ... some of them had terrible, terrifying stories to tell. He had also met a few of the people he had met the second time he had run away, and he had been frightened by the changes that had come over them. Drink—cheap wine and cider—and drugs, glue especially, had eaten away at their minds and bodies. Some of them were so far gone that they couldn't even remember their own names, never mind his.

Spider stopped on O'Connell Bridge as a young man he knew—he couldn't have been more than fourteen or fifteen—staggered by him, his eyes blank and unseeing, a puffed paper bag in his hand. Spider looked at the remains of the burger in his hand and suddenly didn't feel so hungry any more, but he still forced himself to finish the food. He looked back at the young man weaving his way across the bridge, and wondered if this was how he was going to end up—out of his mind on cheap drink or glue.

He sat down on the dirty benches beneath the statue of Daniel O'Connell, and wondered what future there was for him on the streets.

In the early morning light the street was sparkling, looking washed and clean from the night's rain. The two lines of neatly terraced houses facing one another looked odd after the chaos of the city centre, and the boy felt like an alien.

He stood outside the door for several long moments before finally ringing the bell. He had rehearsed his conversation, his little speech, knew what he was going to say.

But when the door finally opened and the small stout woman looked out, he found he could say nothing. The woman looked at the boy, and then she smiled and reached out her hand. When he touched the warm fingertips he found he could speak.

"Hello Mum."

"Welcome home, Spider."

The Longest Day

Ita Daly

The Longest Day
Ita Daly

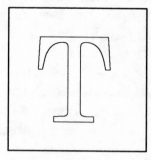oday was the fifth of March and tomorrow Sorcha Drew would be twelve years old. Sorcha was not thinking of tomorrow, however, and the treats which her mother had promised her. She was thinking about this time last year when everything had been so different: when she had been able to wake up in the morning without that horrid feeling of dread descending on her. When she had been happy.

She got out of bed now and began to rummage in the wardrobe for something to wear. This time last year she would have been preoccupied with trying to match up socks and T-shirt and hair band. Today she just wanted to find something clean.

In September when she went to her new

school she would not have to bother about choosing clothes—each school day she would simply step into her green school skirt and white shirt. She couldn't wait for September to come, to get away from all the familiar faces that now surrounded her. In the past it was this aspect of her school which she had loved—knowing everybody so well, teachers and pupils. Now her stomach began to churn as she thought of the look on their faces, their well-intentioned kindness and concern if she had to tell them ...

But maybe it wouldn't come to that, maybe she was just exaggerating everything in her own mind. If only she knew. If only they would tell her something and didn't keep on saying that she was too young and that there was nothing to know anyway.

In the kitchen her mother stood at a worktop filling lunch boxes. She had dark circles under her eyes, and in the unkind March sunshine Sorcha suddenly thought how old she looked.

"Good morning, darling." Her smile wrenched at Sorcha's heart. "Help yourself to some porridge there on the cooker."

At the kitchen table Suzanne was writing

with one hand and shovelling cornflakes into her mouth with the other.

"Where's Dad?" Sorcha asked, sitting down opposite her sister.

"He had to go out early this morning." It was her mother who answered. "But he said he'll pick up the lights for your disco on the way home."

Was it Sorcha's imagination or did Suzanne's eyes meet their mother's in some silent message?

"Why does he always have to be out these days?" Sorcha hated the whine in her voice but couldn't stop herself. "Why do I never see him anymore?"

"Darling, that's not true. Daddy is just very busy at the moment, you must try to understand."

"No, I never see him and when I do he's always cross and tired. What's going on? Why won't anybody tell me anything?"

"That's enough, Sorcha. Just get on with your breakfast like a good girl."

"I'm not hungry."

"Sorcha! Come back."

But she had gone, slamming the kitchen door behind her and forgetting about her lunch box on the worktop.

Half way down the road, Suzanne caught up with her. "You should be a bit more considerate, Sorcha," she said. "Mum has a hard enough time as it is."

Sorcha stopped walking and turned round to face her sister.

"I know that and I have being awful but why won't someone tell me what's going on? You know, Susie—what are you and Mammy always whispering about? And then when I come along you shut up and pretend to be all happy and smiley. Why can't you tell me what's going on?"

Suzanne put an arm round her little sister's shoulder. "There are just some things that you are too young to understand—you must accept that, Sorcha. Look, I must dash or I'll be late for school. Here's your lunch box. See you this evening."

And she was gone, leaving Sorcha to trail along to her own school, feeling cross with herself and her family.

At school, the sun shone through the long classroom window. Sixth class dozed at their desks, chewing the ends of pencils, fiddling with hair and nails. It was always harder to concentrate when the sun poured in.

During English, Mrs Meehan read out Sorcha's essay to the class, saying that it showed a maturity and insight that the others would do well to note.

A year ago such comments would have made Sorcha dizzy with delight. At ten she had decided that she was going to be a writer, for writing was what she did naturally and what gave her most pleasure. Now she couldn't think about the future, she could only hold on to the present, one day at a time.

That was why the essay had been so easy to write. "At least three pages on 'A Frightening Experience'," Mrs Meehan had said, and most of the essays had been about ghosts or accidents by the sea. Sorcha had started off her essay, "My life is a frightening experience because I am afraid of the future and what will happen next."

She had concentrated on her own feelings and had written them down, without, of course, giving any clues as to what caused them. So here was Mrs Meehan praising her understanding and psychology, and her classmates were smirking at the star pupil. Sorcha wished that her essay *had* been as boring as theirs. They wrote boring essays, they complained because their lives were boring, as hers used to be. She, too, had once complained, not recognising happiness until it had been taken from her.

How she and Suzanne used to give out about those weekend drives, always either to Dun Laoire or Howth. Dad would sit behind the wheel, humming along to the car radio, while Mum would turn round and say, "Cheer up, you two. Before you know where you are these family outings will be a thing of the past and it's only then that you'll miss them."

Sorcha would never have believed that those words would come true so quickly.

There were other aspects of their old life that had bored her too, mainly to do with its predictability, the even rhythm of each day. Nothing exciting ever happens to this family, she used to tell herself, in fact nothing ever happens at all.

Now, something was happening, and with a vengeance, and Sorcha had been made to realize that boredom was infinitely preferable to pain.

At Break, she stayed in, pretending that

she wasn't feeling well. She often did that or asked Mrs Meehan if there was any job she could do around the classroom. When the bell rang and the others came streaming in, she was back at her desk, her head bent over her Irish spelling list. She waited until the chattering had died down, a signal that Mrs Meehan was back at her desk. Then she raised her head, knowing that she was safe for another while from her classmates' pitying glances and curious eyes.

She tried hard to concentrate during Irish, and again during maths. Again and again however, her thoughts kept straying, and she wasn't surprised when a few minutes before the end of lessons, Mrs Meehan summoned her up to her desk.

"Would you mind staying behind for a second, Sorcha?" she asked. "There's something I want to ask you."

The other children looked at her as they sidled out the door, some of them making signs of support, as if they imagined she was really for it now.

"Right," said Mrs Meehan as the door closed behind the last of them. "Sit down here, Sorcha, and we'll have a little chat.

Would you like a cup of coffee—I could get
one from the staff-room?"

"No thanks, Mrs Meehan." This didn't
sound as if she were going to start a dressing-
down.

"All right then. Sorcha—is there anything
troubling you? I can't help noticing that you
seem a bit upset sometimes and I was just
wondering—"

"No, there's nothing troubling *me*, Mrs
Meehan." Sorcha raised her head and stared
straight into her teacher's eyes.

"Everything all right at home?"

"Oh yes, Mrs Meehan."

Mrs Meehan paused and looked out the
window, then she turned back to Sorcha.
"You know you could tell me if there was
anything troubling you and it wouldn't go
any farther. That's part of my job, seeing that
my pupils are happy If you're not happy, you
can't learn."

"But there's nothing to tell—I'm perfectly
happy."

"Oh Sorcha, anyone can see that's not true.
I mean, you used to be so good at all your
subjects—you were always right at the top of
the class. But recently you don't even seem

interested anymore and you look so sad sometimes ... What is it, Sorcha? You can tell me."

Sorcha could feel her heart beating rapidly inside her chest. Mrs Meehan mustn't find out—she mustn't even suspect. She could imagine her pity. And no matter what she said, once *she* had found out, the others would soon know. Like a cornered animal Sorcha knew that her only defence was to attack. She re-arranged her features and looked up at Mrs Meehan with as much insolence as she could manage.

"I suppose it never occurred to you, Mrs Meehan, that your classes could be deadly boring, that I've outgrown them and you? There's nothing the matter with me or my home. I'm just bored to death with this school."

"Well!"

Sorcha watched as Mrs Meehan's face turned first white and then a painful red.

"Why—you horrible little girl! How dare you speak to me like that. I can see now how mistaken I've been in you. And to think that I should have wasted so much time worrying about you. Well, let that be a lesson to me."

She stood up and began buttoning up her cardigan. "You may leave the room. Immediately."

Sorcha picked up her schoolbag, and without raising her eyes from the floor quietly let herself out and gently closed the door behind her.

She felt even more miserable now, for she had seen the expression of hurt on Mrs Meehan's face. And Sorcha liked this teacher who had always been kind and interested in all of her pupils, but perhaps with a special soft spot for Sorcha.

Sorcha had never before given cheek to a teacher, even in fifth class when she had hated Miss Ryan, who was feared throughout the school for her sarcastic tongue.

And today she had attacked poor Mrs Meehan who had never shown her anything but kindness. But she had no option—she had needed to protect her secret and her home.

She had sacrificed a great deal to protect her secret. Now when she came out into the schoolyard, there was nobody waiting for her. The others had all gone home. If this had happened last year Anna Lee would have been waiting, as she had on every such occasion since junior infants. They had started school together and Sorcha's mother and Anna's father had decided on that first day that their two daughters *had* to be soulmates, the only two infants who had stood at the school door, bawling their heads off, refusing to enter. For seven and a half years that friendship had survived. Anna had been loyal throughout those years, and Sorcha had repaid that loyalty by simply turning her back on her friend without a word of explanation. All to protect her secret.

"Sorry, I'm busy this week-end." "I don't want to see that film." "I'd rather do my homework on my own, if you don't mind. I get more done that way."

Anna had got the message quick enough, and for the last month she hadn't rung once. Now, she avoided Sorcha in school and had taken up with Julie Donoghue. But she couldn't stop herself from throwing the occasional reproachful glance across the class-room at her one-time friend.

"I don't know what's got into you," Sorcha's mother had said. "You've even driven away poor Anna. You really should try not to be so bad-tempered."

When her mother wasn't lecturing her, Suzanne was; in fact the only one who ever threw her a kind word these days was her father. She didn't see much of him, but at least he didn't bite her head off when he was around. They had always been mates,—she had been Daddy's girl, as Suzanne was Mammy's. They shared interests, history and cycling, and they had the same sense of humour. Not that either of them had done much laughing recently.

She couldn't imagine life without him. As this thought struck, she felt the familiar sense of panic fill her chest. She took a deep breath and told herself to be sensible. She had too much imagination, that was her problem. Understandable and even desirable in one who wanted to be a writer.

That was it! She had been merely telling herself stories, imagining, exaggerating, noting down tiny events that other more down-to-earth types would overlook completely.

Perhaps it was just as her mother had said and that now, as Sorcha was on the threshold of adolescence, she was suddenly feeling insecure and life was becoming difficult for her. Maybe all adolescents suffered from these fantasies, these dark imaginings, as their lives opened up and the certainties of childhood fell away. She had always been a worrier—now it had just grown more acute.

She was almost happy as she walked home. She began to notice the world which she hadn't seen for months. She felt the sun warm on her back and swung her schoolbag slowly. She wondered suddenly, "What's for tea?" and hoped that there might be chips. As she walked up her front path, Mr Donnolly nodded over the next-door fence.

"Spring's arrived," he said, leaning on a rake. "I've given the grass its first cut, Sorcha. What do you think of that?"

She let herself in and stood for a moment in the dim hallway. "I'm home," she called. Silence. "I'm home," she said again, bursting into the kitchen in time to see Suzanne and her mother draw their heads apart.

Her sense of well-being evaporated. She didn't imagine the tension in the air, the strained expressions on their faces that now turned towards her.

"I'll just go on up to my room," she said

before either of them could speak. "I've a lot of homework to do."

The fantasy had been in allowing herself to believe that everything was all right. Reality had a dull familiar feel about it.

When she heard her father's car, she didn't at first pay it any heed until, glancing at her watch, she realized that it was only half past five. Normally he didn't return home until about six and recently it had been much later. Could this be a good omen then?

She finished her sums and was in the bathroom washing her hands when Suzanne called out, "Tea's ready, Sorcha."

The kitchen seemed different, or maybe it was the people who were in it. They sat at the table, backs straight, nobody talking. They turned to look at her as she walked in and for some reason she found herself blushing.

"I've made spaghetti bolognese," her mother said. "I know how popular it is with you two and I've been thinking how dull the food's been in this house recently."

There was a bottle of wine on the table, something that never occurred except on special occasions, special celebrations. Sorcha felt a sudden lightness round her heart, as if a great weight had been lifted. Her father's early return coupled with the bottle of wine must mean something good.

"Hey," she said, settling in beside Suzanne, "what are we celebrating?"

Her father coughed and her mother looked down at her hands.

"We *are* celebrating, aren't we?"

After a pause, her mother replied. "Not exactly Sorcha ... not celebrating."

"Then—?"

"It's just that Daddy and I have something we want to discuss with you and we thought ..." Her voice died away and she looked appealingly at her younger daughter.

"We were going to wait until after your birthday," her father said. "But then we thought it was better coming beforehand, so's at least you'd have the party to look forward to."

Sorcha stood up abruptly, knocking over her chair. "I don't want to listen. There's nothing you can tell me that I want to hear."

She turned to flee but her father's voice stopped her. "Pick up your chair Sorcha and sit down." He never spoke to her like that, in such a stern tone. She looked at his face and it was white with lines around the mouth that she had never noticed before. Quietly she retrieved her chair and sat back at the table.

"Your mother and I have decided—" his words were interrupted by her mother.

"Darling," she took Sorcha's hand. "You're twelve tomorrow and you're growing up fast. What you're going to hear is not going to be easy for you but you must be brave. Daddy and I have decided—we can't—we've tried—"

"What your mother is trying to say is that we are going to live apart from now on."

"Jim, *please*. You must try to understand, Sorcha. We have tried, both of us, but we've come to the conclusion that the only solution, for all our sakes, is that we two separate."

"It's not for my sake," Sorcha withdrew her hand. "Spare me the lies at least."

"For heaven's sake, Sorcha," Suzanne glared at her. "Grow up."

But Sorcha was past listening to advice from her sister or from anybody else. If grown-ups behaved like this then she had no particular desire to copy them. She felt tears well up and spill hotly down her cheeks.

"But why can't you live together, why can't

you? Don't you love one another any more? You've always said how much you loved one another—what's happened? Has Daddy found a girl friend or—is it my fault? Was it all my disobediences that—"

Her mother took in her arms. "You mustn't think that, Sorcha." She passed her to her father's arms and he took her on his knee and began to dry her tears with his big, white handkerchief. "It was nothing to do with you or with anybody else, it's just that sometimes, these things happen. We can't live together anymore—we're tearing one another apart— you've heard us often enough, God knows. We've had a wonderful marriage and we have two beautiful daughters and I'll always be your father and continue to love you as much as I do now. And I love your mother too, but we just have to separate."

"Daddy, I won't let you." She flung her arms around his neck. "I won't let you leave."

"My suitcase is packed, Sorcha. You must be brave."

He spoke quietly so that it seemed to Sorcha as if the beating of her heart was drowning out his words. "But Daddy—not— when—?"

"Tonight, Sorcha. There's no point in hanging around."

It was very quiet. The sodium light from the street filled the bedroom with a dirty orange glow. Sorcha turned her head towards her clock radio. Five minutes to twelve.

Daddy had gone soon after nine, saying that he would be back tomorrow to organize her disco. Suzanne had made tea then and the three of them had sat round the table where the tea things still lay unwashed. Her mother had said nothing but Suzanne had given her sister a pep talk: she was old enough to understand these things, they would both see their father on a regular basis and they must try to pull their weight and be as helpful as possible. Her mother had started crying then and even Suzanne had shed a tear.

"We won't set any alarms tonight," Mammy had said as they'd crawled up the stairs shortly after eleven. "Nobody need get up early tomorrow."

Sorcha however had set her alarm. She would go to school tomorrow after she had taken her mother a cup of tea and she would tell her friends and Mrs Meehan what had happened. And she would have her party with the disco.

Funnily enough she didn't feel quite as bad now as she had this morning. The worst had happened and she had to deal with it. And she could. She had grown up a lot in the last five or six hours. The worst had happened but life would go on and had to be lived.

She yawned and turned to look at the clock again. Two minutes past twelve. The day was over and thank God for that.

It had been the longest day of her life.

Struggles of a Storyteller

Mary Beckett

Struggles of a Storyteller
Mary Beckett

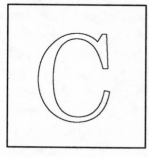

laire appeared for her breakfast one Thursday in her usual uniform for school—wrinkled knee-socks, sloppy black shoes, longish skirt, and pullover with chewed looking sleeves hanging well over her hands. "You'll need your trousers," her mother said. "It's beginning to snow."

"I'm not wearing jeans to school," Claire protested. "I'm not allowed."

"Well you're not allowed to go out of here on your bicycle without them and your coat buttoned up and your hat and gloves."

"Sister Stanislaus says anybody cycling in trousers is to take them off outside the school gate."

"Massive traffic-jam on Elmwood Avenue," her brother jeered as he got ready for his school, just up the road. "Striptease by St. Lucy's girls."

Her mother insisted and indeed Claire counted herself lucky to get out without waterboots as well. By the time she reached Elmwood Avenue the snow was thick and the cars were crawling. She hoped nobody would notice her when she propped her bicycle against the hedge opposite the big old gates of the school and tried to pull off her jeans. Her fingers were frozen and she didn't want to stagger a shoe-less foot into the snow, so she hadn't managed much when a long black car stopped just beside her because the car in front seemed to have stalled. The big car belonged to one of the Arab embassies. Yasmin something-or-other, an ambassador's daughter, was driven to school every day by a chauffeur. She was two years ahead of Claire and was very beautiful. But out of the rear door of the car scrambled Dolores Duffy who was in second year with Claire, who was not a bit beautiful but was earnest and quiet.

Usually she was brought to school by her elderly father who walked her there and back with his big black umbrella. He had once banged on the front of Claire's father's car with that umbrella because he thought the car might move while Dolores was crossing the road. Claire's father had not been too pleased. The Arabs must have offered Dolores a lift because of the snow. Her house was near the embassy. It was typical of her that she couldn't sit in the car to be delivered at the school door; she would have to be humble and no bother, Claire was thinking uncharitably, when two men with hooded anoraks got out of the car behind, grabbed Dolores, pushed her into the car in front and drove off in it. The chauffeur turned in through the school gate, peering through the snow, noticing nothing.

Claire stood gaping for a minute and then pulled her clothes together, got up on her bike and followed the car. It was not diffiuclt because the traffic was so slow and although her bike skidded a few times she kept up well enough to see the car unload Dolores and three men at the gate of an old three-storey house in Inkermann Road and then drive away. She got the number but she couldn't think what she should do next. There was no sense in her going up to the door. What could she do with all those men? She supposed she'd better inform the guards. After several wrong turns she found her way, wet, cold and bedraggled to the garda station. She went inside hesitantly. She had never been inside a police station before.

"Well, what is it?" a guard at a desk asked her without looking up. "Bicycle stolen? Purse lost?"

Claire cleared her throat and squeaked "A girl was kidnapped."

"Are you doing this for a dare?" he frowned at her. "We're busy you know, young lady. Clear off home now or to school or wherever you should be." Another guard announced that Ranelagh was blocked with traffic and that there were minor accidents on Aylesbury Road so nobody took any more interest in Claire, who lost heart. She began to wonder had she seen what she thought she'd seen at all. She headed back to school, confident that the nuns would be able to handle it.

She met parents' cars blocking the gate. "School's closed until Monday," somebody shouted. Claire stood in the shelter of the big gate pillar, nearly crying with the cold, wondering what she should do and how she was to cycle away over to Templeogue in the

snow which was now lying thickly on the
ground and blowing almost a blizzard. When
Jane O'Rawe put her head out of her
mother's Peugeot station wagon and called
"Come on Claire! Put your bike in the back
and Mum will take you to our house," she did
as she was told. Jane had been at the school
since she was five and her mother was a past
pupil so Jane was very self-confident. She
knew where everything was in the school and
she even called Sister Stanislaus "Stan"
practically to her face. Besides, she was slim
and had good skin. Her mother looked smart
in her track suit, younger than Claire's
mother.

"Can we drop you off at your house?" she
asked.

"Oh no, Mum. Claire lives absolutely miles
away."

"I can ride home from here," Claire said,
not wanting to be a bother.

"Not at all," Mrs. O'Rawe said. "You'll come
to our house and we'll phone your mother.
Maybe somebody could collect you? Or if the
snow eases you'll be able to ride home before
dark."

"My father's in Cork with the car," Claire

explained miserably.

"Then you'll have lunch with us" Mrs. O'Rawe said. "You're frozen."

The car gave a bit of a skid so that she had to concentrate on her driving and Claire tried to tell Jane about Dolores being kidnapped.

"Oh Claire, you do tell such great stories," Jane laughed and Claire left it at that because it was better to be a great story-teller than a great idiot.

At the house Mrs. O'Rawe put the car into the garage and told Claire to put her bike beside it.

"I can't see myself having that out again today," she said and Claire's heart sank. The house was big. Jane and her younger sister had a bedroom each, unlike Claire who shared a room with her two sisters in bunks. They found clothes for Claire—a track suit, dry socks, slippers. They drank Nescafe round the pine table in the elegant kitchen and ate chocolate biscuits. When she was warm and comfortable she telephoned her mother, who was worrying about her. She warned Claire to be no trouble to anyone and to thank Mrs. O'Rawe properly for being so kind to her, and she hoped to see her before dark but she sounded dubious. She wanted to speak to Mrs. O'Rawe. Claire heard Mrs. O'Rawe assure her that she was delighted to have her to keep Jane and Sarah from fighting, and if she had to stay the night they had a spare bedroom, but snow rarely lasted and it would probably melt in the afternoon.

They ate chicken breast taken out of the freezer and cooked in the microwave, and tomato and onion simmered with garlic, and rice. Claire thought it was the most opulent meal she'd ever eaten. Chicken in her house was stuffed and roasted and then all sliced up so that each of the six could have a fair share. Mrs. O'Rawe did not eat with them. She took a cup of coffee and a slimming biscuit into the drawing room. Claire was delighted with the company of the two sisters. She told them about a French aunt she'd invented for herself in the Beaujolais region near Lyons, who was anxious to have her for the Summer holidays. She told them about a Jewish grandmother living glamorously in London. The colour supplements of the English Sunday newspapers were a great source for her imaginings. She described as her own a bedroom furnished by Habitat. And all the time she worried about Dolores. "Should we ring Duffy's house?" she suggested. "Just to see if Dolores got home." Jane laughed and said "Why not!"

Sarah asked if Claire always ended up believing her own stories. Jane pushed her. All three went into the hall to phone but the telephone was dead and not long afterwards the electricity went.

When Dominic O'Rawe came in laughing at four o'clock from his school, which hadn't shut, flung his school bag down in the hall and changed his long sixteen year-old legs into jeans and runners, he could get nothing hot to eat. He wolfed the greater part of a loaf of bread, cut in thick slices and weighted with butter and jam. He put the milk bottle to his mouth and finished it in two goes. Claire thought he was wonderful. She didn't mind at all that he spoke with his mouth full even though she was always begging her mother to improve her own brother's manners. He rushed out afterwards to snowball his friends. The house grew cold and Mrs O'Rawe told them to light an old bottle-gas heater in the television room. She said she was going to her mother's house to see how she was managing, and if their father by any chance came home they were to send him there.

"Granny will have a fire," Sarah said. "And she has a gas cooker."

"Hadn't you better get out candles?" Claire asked, knowing that was what they did at home. They always had lost of candles, all kinds of bits and stumps in saucers and jampots. Jane brought in two silver candlesticks from the dining room with tall green candles and set them up in the television room but when Dominic came in, the rest of the house was dark. He stamped in and seized one out of its candlestick and rampaged up to his room shouting about how cold and wet he was. The thought came into Claire's head that he was showing off and she felt very pleased. The candle light made them all look much prettier.

"What'll we do?" Sarah said. Claire suggested a game where one person began to tell a story and the next person had to take it up and the next and the next making it funny or exciting. Claire's family often played it when, after quarrels over the television, their mother came in and turned it off with the

edict "No more television until tomorrow."
The O'Rawes, not being used to the game,
were not very imaginative, not even Dominic.
When Claire proposed "Sister Rebecca died
last night," they picked that up much better
and ended falling about laughing. Dominic
found an old Rubik cube and demonstrated
how clever he was at that. They played
Scrabble when they discovered it, barely
used, at the back of the cupboard, but they
did not treat it earnestly so Claire didn't
mind that she could not get very far with it.

"I could bring down my chess set," Dominic
said. "Can you play chess, Claire?"

Claire said she could but his two sisters
said, "No, Dominic, we're not going to sit
quiet while you play chess."

Claire was relieved because she was afraid
she was not good enough.

"We must have a game some other time,"
Dominic said to her and brought in the rest of
the biscuits and a carton of orange juice.

There were no hot water bottles and no hot
baths. Claire in her borrowed nightdress was
cold as she washed her face and hands, and
congratulated herself that she always had
her toothbrush in her schoolbag. In bed she

curled up her feet to warm herself and prayed that she'd be able to go home in the morning. It was all wonderful and exciting but a bit of a strain. She also prayed that poor Dolores was safe at home with her father, who looked so worried even when there was nothing to worry about. She was wakened early by the electric light because somebody had left it switched on the previous day. She could hear the constant drip, drip that meant there was a thaw and she lay impatiently until nearly eight o'clock when she heard someone stirring. She dressed quickly, disgusted that she had to wear yesterday's unwashed clothes.

Dominic in his school uniform was in the kitchen setting a tray with two little triangles of toast and a teapot. "Hello," he said. "I'll get our breakfast in a minute. That's if you'd like me to. This is Mum's. Dad does this if he's here but he didn't get home last night. If Dad's not here I do it."

"It looks lovely," Claire said in real admiration. When he came downstairs he made a stack of buttered toast and laid the table for the two of them.

"I didn't think girls got up early," he said

"Jane and Sarah will be in bed till lunchtime."

"I'm going home," Claire said. "It's not rude just to leave a note to say thanks, is it? I don't want my father having to come for me. Will you help me get my bike from the garage?

"Of course I will." His manners were perfect. "What age are you?" he asked suddenly and when Claire said she was nearly fourteen he went on. "That would make you old enough for me to take you to my debs in two years time, wouldn't it? Do you think you could come?"

"Oh yes, I'd love to!" Claire said, her head spinning with joy.

"It's better to have it all arranged well ahead," Dominic explained, "then you don't have to think about it and worry about it. It doesn't interfere then with your rugby or even your homework."

Claire rode home through the slush. The middle of the road was wet where the cars whooshed by, but at the sides where bicycles went, brown water was trapped between compressed lumps of dingy snow. Claire was filthy by the time she arrived at her own gate where the paths had been cleared. Her feet and hands were soaked and frozen but she was happy with life and happy to be home.

"Oh Claire, I am glad to see you. We missed you all the time," her mother greeted her. "But you need a bath first. Then you can tell me your adventures." The kitchen range warmed the whole house. Her mother would have cooked a hot meal on it last night as usual. Claire's untidy half a bedroom cluttered with books and tapes and silly soft toys was welcoming, as always.

As she soaked in the hot water she wondered if the phone was working yet. Not that she would have had the nerve to ring the guards again. It was strange that, even without looking at her properly, the guard knew that she was given to making up stories. She wished she could tell her mother but she could well imagine her satirical eye, and the rest of the family would only laugh at her. She made up her mind to stick, from that moment, to the absolute truth. She could try ringing Dolores's house again.

She had to wait until Monday. She arrived early and was so pleased to see Dolores looking exactly the same as ever that she alarmed her by her dash across the cloakroom. "Oh Dolores! Are you all right? What happened after you went into that house?" At first Dolores pursed up her mouth. Then she said in a low voice: "The guards don't want anybody to know until they catch the men. Anyway, as soon as they found out I wasn't Yasmin they drove me straight home. I was home before the school was closed." She laughed quietly.

All the time I was trailing around on the bike and being insulted in the garda station she was warm and dry, Claire thought, but she said nothing. Jane O'Rawe came in and saw the two of them with their heads together.

"Is she trying to make you go along with her story, Dolores? You should have heard all the excitement she had you involved in. Come on Dolores and I'll tell you." They moved off. When Claire ran after them to give Jane the thank-you letter for her mother, Jane took it without looking at her. Dolores was the heroine, even though, as far as Jane knew, the adventure had only happened in a story.

Claire's own friend, Biddie, late as usual, flung her arms round Claire. "We thought you might be lost in the snow." Claire hadn't remembered her during the whole week-end event though they had sat together for over a year, except when the teachers separated them for talking in class.

"I stayed in Jane O'Rawe's house," Claire said.

"Oh I say! Very grand," Biddie said, rolling her eyes.

"Very kind. Really. They were very good to me," Claire said, thinking how prim she sounded. She could not talk about the O'Rawes because she had been their guest. She could not tell about Dolores since that was supposed to be secret. And she could not make up marvellous happenings because she'd promised herself never to do that again.

For a moment she thought life was going to be drab. Then while they trooped up to class Biddie was talking away and she congratulated herself on having her for a friend. Besides, she had a nice enough family who always coped. Best of all, she had two years to enjoy looking forward to St. Augustine's debs with Dominic O'Rawe. She hoped he would remember.

Rosaleen Rafferty at Rosario's Tech

Evelyn Conlon

Rosaleen Rafferty
at Rosario's Tech.
Evelyn Conlon

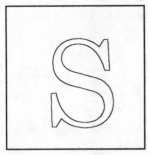

he should have known
when he said, smiling,
for the third time dur-
ing the interview "A lot of our boys join the
Army." She did actually. But then she should
have known that Ben meant it when he said
"If you make an ass out of me like that again,
out you go on you ear." She did actually, but
at least smiley boots here was going to give
her the job. She could tell. She said smiley
boots in order to give herself confidence.

"When can you start, Miss Rafferty?" "Ms."
"Sorry?" "Ms.—Ms. Rafferty." His face shot
into a clap of thunder. His cheek bone was
twitching as he let her out the door.

I've blown it, she said to herself, then
thought, maybe we could come to an
arrangement—I'll ignore his tic if he ignores

my unreasonable desire to be addressed like
a human being, forgetting for a minute that
she wasn't one of the arrangers. A tangle-
weed of depression rose up at the gate-posts
and wrapped itself around her throat,
making her gasp for air. Air, as bad as it was,
was better than choking.

So started Rosaleen Rafferty on a
skimming spree across the minds of the
pupils of Rosario's Tech for Boys.

During the first few weeks she got sick in
the mornings. She was frightened by the nest
of open mouths in front of her; no names, no
idea of what to do if they spat at the
blackboard when her back was turned, which
they sometimes did. But within a week she
was ready to start each day. She would prove
that there could be more for them than their
perceived lot. She would like them, like them,
even if it killed her. By God, she would like
them.

By now she knew who was who, who
couldn't read at all, who was the meanest
person on this whole earth, who couldn't do
joined up writing, who lived in the
orphanage, whose father was in jail. The
staff-room verdict was really a plea. What

would you expect? He's from a broken home. Rosaleen found out that the ones from the smithereened houses more often than not were the very ones who had one room standing for themselves.

The boys would have liked her to be marmy so they could stick pins in her or spit at the blackboard but she knew better. She would tighten the rules of love, throw them out, pull them in. She might even make these boys smile at her. They hadn't seen too much of that—this was not a school with happy teachers. There was no kindness in its corridors. Even in their own room the teachers were afraid. But in her room things were beginning to change. She had made two disparaging remarks about the Army. Ben would have been proud of how she had slipped them in.

The boys were cold in the mornings. They stood like single blades of grass frozen stiff. They breathed stale air. If one of their breaths crossed another's he was as likely to get a thump as a sneer. The sneers would have mashed any delicate hearts if they had not already been turned into punch bags. By nine-thirty the thaw was setting in. The toughs had escaped from whatever bit of innocence sleep had forced on them. The boys who were determined to forge a character for themselves had begun to test bits of it out on each other, on her. This testing, herein surely lay the secret.

The sky was pickled with frost one morning. It would have been a decisive day if this had been the country. A no-nonsense-sharp-do-what-you-have-to-do day.

The frost bit into Rosaleen's despair, wakening her up. Today will be good. By God, today will be good. She hopped over the weed at the gate. "We will all write about an ordinary day in our lives." Half a dozen boys grunted, at least ten nipped or punched each other, the rest ignored her. "As I said, we will write about an ordinary day." That's twice she said that, "Me as well. I will start my essay by saying ..." She got a sudden, daring silence. *O.K., come on Miss say something interesting to us, surprise us, come on, Miss.* The next ten seconds would decide which way the silence was to go. "I will start my essay by saying ..." "But Miss, nothing happens us." David and Leo remembered, together, some unsolved insult—*hey you, just you wait, pigface.* The two boys searched frantically for the words they hated most, splittering insults that would do until they could find the worst possible one, "... by saying, last night I rang my boyfriend, my ex-boyfriend, again. I knew he was out. I just rang to hear his voice on the answering machine. He still had my name on the tape."

Complete silence.

"There's a blank page. This minute you are no-one, or at least we don't see you. Build yourselves there, paint your own picture." They started to mutter but were still confused. *Had she really said that?* Before they'd finished mumbling, she had placed a blank page on each desk. A separate page made it more important than their own copybooks. "As I was saying, his voice hadn't changed at all."

"How long ago since you'd heard it, Miss."

"Three months Liam. Now! You can start your ordinary day by talking about the sounds of voices in the morning. Who speaks first, who likes to be quiet in the morning." *If anyone*, she muttered to herself.

"But Miss, we told you nothing happens us."

"Well, nothing happened to me last night except ..." she offered.

"Ah, go on Miss, tell us."

"Except I watched television, corrected your essays and ..."

"And what Miss." The leer was gathering steam.

"We will see when all your essays are done."

She looked at them. What could they do? She had won. They would write now, not because it was of any use to them—what use are stupid essays, but because they wanted to find out what she had the nerve to write. A teacher! "Now don't worry about my essay, think about your own." What have you the nerve to write. She could be a good mind reader. Oh! it was a great week. She made them re-write and they did so gladly because they began to believe her; this was them. They handed her pieces each day—letters pinched with cold, letters open as bowls, letters pleading to the sky, letters already hardened into stone.

But then David Lean's father wrote his own piece and it landed into their classroom like a nasty missile from outside, dragging them back to the meagreness of the acceptable. *Dear Miss, I'll not have you getting my son to write out everything we are doing here. I know what's going on, trying to nose your way into our house. You do your job during school and I'll do mine after in my own house.* He also sent a copy to the Headmaster. She couldn't hide it from the boys either, because David Lean, not knowing what else to do, had already swelled out telling them in the school-yard before the morning bell went. The rest of them didn't know why but they went with David and his father, because how could they not? Against her, the teacher. They mumbled all that day in class. They would not write. On the way out Mark Turner said "and you never showed us the last of yours Miss." "Good on ya, Twamsey" came from one of the back voices that was now pushing the others. "Stop pushing fatface."

"I was going to," she said, and meant it.

The Headmaster said the the Army was not the sort of place where you spend your time thinking about ordinary days. He tried to say it with some light-heartedness, the softest Rosaleen ever saw him, but she snorted. After she was outside the gate.

And so the class went back to its original battlefield. Rosaleen stole minutes to catch her breath, when the boys momentarily forgot to fight themselves or her. Watching their bent heads she could imagine innocent things living there. Seven fours Miss? Twenty eight, Miss. She had always seen numbers as standing there in rows, beginning east, one to twenty. Twenty to thirty, east to west. Thirty to forty, west to east. So when she would get to aged twenty the hardest part would be over. Did any of them see numbers like this?

Why was there no one to take a picture of her standing here in front of her adversaries? Them quiet now. How unbelievably quiet. How many seconds would it last? Should she be thinking of something to do when they would inevitably lift their heads, something to stop them from tearing this room apart? Like them? She was afraid of them. People have less important pictures taken, ones at the boat in Dub Laoghaire, that could be anywhere, ones at parties that were forgotten before the film got developed, ones holding hands that would mock them from the bottom of the pile unless they were unsuperstitious enough to burn them. Why not a picture of her here?

No one ever saw this—a teacher, a lone teacher, five foot three, against twenty five boys, one hundred and thirty one feet six. There was a photo of her and Ben. They looked well, with his head on her shoulder. But that wasn't true—she had pulled his head down on her shoulder a minute before the flash went, just so they could have one picture where they looked as if they liked each other; one photograph wasn't too much to set up, and the smile on his face was really from surprise at what she'd just done. Why couldn't they let her daydream, even for a few minutes? How could they fight her even on that? How could they fight such a mercurial thing? Day-dreaming was important. They could drop out any time to daydream. If she noticed she certainly never drew their attention back; they might learn more in that faraway place, and even if they did not, it kept them quiet. But her, oh no, they'd never let her daydream.

She drew her eyes back and they looked at her. They had been looking at her, for how long? Oh the dears, the little lovely dears, they had been camera enough. "Thank you boys." "It's all right Miss, any time." She and they laughed.

But the next morning something else ugly had planted itself in the room. She could smell it when she came in. She could never be sure what it was, or how bad it was going to be, only that it was there. The air crackled. That meant the intercom. They stopped slicing at each other and gave one minute's attention. The Headmaster's voice was clear, uncivilian. *Three of our past pupils were killed last night. You will all attend Mass at lunchtime.* The intercom switched off. He hadn't said their names.

There was a minute's silence and then words spoken in hushed, angry voices. And this new inconsideration, mixed in with whatever was there before, sent boys hurling at each other. Why should they care? If he had come around each classroom, and spoken the names, it would have been different, Rosaleen said to herself. Why should she care? Let them murder each other. She couldn't possibly come between them anyway. Was it for this that she had put in years of learning how to learn and then learning how to teach, that she had in the beginning suffered humilations that came up in welts on her body when she slept?

There was one immune boy, Liam. He had sprouted ideas early, and now he was in love. With a girl called Rosemary. He was having his first summer although it was February. Why had this never happened before? Why Rosemary? What was it? He had built for himself a private dream around his desk—it had a town in it, songs, people to pass on his way up the road where he would see her. Sometimes he tried to concentrate on history—it was his favourite subject— Rosaleen would have not believed that there could be such a thing as a favourite subject in this class room—but once a key word fell, there were thousands of them. And then he would lose the grip of solid daily things and find himself being cajoled up the street again.

Rosaleen wanted to be able to go home to Ben. It used to be that she could go to him and talk about the ozone layer, or some such disaster, or poor Salman Rushdie, or the poor Muslim women as well, we'd better not forget them, and also the fact that, let's not forget, our fingers aren't clean either, and he'd put his arms around her and say nothing is going to happen, you're just a worrier; and she'd believe him that nothing was going to happen.

In the morning Rosaleen was too tired to care. She would stand here and let them kill themselves if they wanted to. The noise whispered below the surface, the boys sniffed a lot, the noise gathered like a steam roller. She looked out the window past their faces which she found just too raw today. She fixed her eyes on the only piece of grass to be seen from these windows, in fact from the entire school. No matter how you craned your neck from no matter which place, you couldn't see grass. It was so small, so far away, she was never quite sure if it was grass. What if it was someone's roof and they painted it red some weekend? She narrowed her eyes and pushed her way over the miles, forcing herself to see flowers pushing up.

The noise began to thump, it was going to crack. She said, to the square of grass, in a low oily voice: "Gentlemen, will you please be quiet." She could have slipped on the words. "Gentlemen," and the word created its own noise. Not one of them dared resist it. And it became apparent that she meant it, because she continued to look at the grass. Some of them looked out the window, following her eyes, but they could see nothing. They fiddled, giggled, only a little, passed notes to each other, drew pictures, shocked that this could be asked of them. When the bell went they said "Miss can we go now?" Although they didn't want to go. "Yes," she said.

And in the morning she believed in them. Could this be the same class? She could see into them, they were full of hearts, veins, livers, they had toes, foreheads and elbows; they liked her, they wanted her to teach them things, they thought those things important. Those things were important, Geography. But they weren't too interested where Balbriggan or Maynooth were, she could tell. She said "I'll not have you making asses of yourselves with girls from all over the country"—they'd never thought of girls all over the country before—"I'll not have you saying you're from Tralee, really, we went on holidays to Roscommon once." So she cleared the desks to the outer edge of the room and stood them in lines and gave them hands to point to where the places were and she gave them girls to match the places. Sally Shovelin from Sligo, Bethina Toal from Tyrone, Kitsy Kinnane from Kerry. Then she sat them down and they drew themselves on maps in Rosarios Tech for Boys, and they filled in their girls' names and places and what those girls' lives were like in those particular places.

May I ask, Miss Rafferty, what your class was doing standing in line all over the classroom when they should have been sitting?

Practising for the Army.

Five minutes late and the rain lashing down. Six minutes late. *Now if he finds this out he'll have one up his sleeve for months. What's that line outside the door?* As Rosaleen got closer, and closer, she could pick out boys. Her class. Their clothes, skimpy, too thin, too small jackets, or just jumpers, soaked into them. Their hair streaking with wet. The hungrier ones shivering. "What's the meaning of this?"

"Well Miss you didn't turn up on time. Look what's happened to us." She could hear tears of cold as much as of rage in their voices.

"Miss Rafferty. In future the classes will stay outside in the morning until their teacher arrives. So it will be in the interest of the teacher to come on time."

"What if they get soaking wet?" "I got the idea yesterday when I saw your class standing in such neat rows."

For the rest of the day Rosaleen stood with her head at the square window in the door. She wanted to keep her nose pressed to it. She wanted to stick her tongue out at him every time he passed.

"Miss Rafferty, I wouldn't worry too much about it," he would say to her face, "it's good training."

"Like the Army I suppose?"

"You seem to have an inordinate dislike for the Army, why would that be? They do at least get trained."

"Trained my eye! Driving around the country, cooped in vans, after money, or lying in ditches along the border with black shoe polish on their faces."

Rosaleen wrote on the blackboard.

Prisons, Crime and Punishment
Why NOT to get into trouble.

"Why not to get caught, Miss?"

"You can discuss that yourselves. I'm not your moral guardian. I just want to tell you why not to get into trouble. And while we are at this we should be able to squeeze in a bit of history."

South to North
Cork
Limerick
Portlaoise
Mountjoy
Arbour Hill
Loughan House
Armagh

now

Maghaberry
Magilligan Camp
Long Kesh
Crumlin Road

"And once there was a ship too," she finished, moving to the back of the class. They all looked at the list. "It's an awful lot of prisons Miss."

And several more besides, she muttered

quietly.

That's where she was standing when he walked in, so she couldn't get to the board to wipe off the evidence. His eyes took in that she hadn't left out the contentious ones. He called her to the door. "Interesting *display* on you blackboard, Miss Rafferty."

"I thought they'd need to know where they are, for when they join the Army, Sir."

"Excuse me for interrupting," he said to the boys.

He beckoned, "Miss Rafferty, take your books home with you. And could you clear your locker out thoroughly. We are going to paint it at the weekend, and we don't want any of your things hanging around.

"Just mine?" she asked, smiling.

"Just yours."